Hauntology

Twenty Supernatural Short Stories

Andrew S. French

Neonoir Books

Also by Andrew S. French

Science Fiction

The Time Traveller's Murder

The Mercy Sleep

Bodies

Another Girl, Another Planet

The Thief of Time Trilogy

The Queens of Heaven

The Queens of Time

The Queens of Space

The Arcane Supernatural Thriller Series

The Arcane

The Arcane Identity

The Arcane Quest

The Arcane Ultimatum

The Ella Finn Fantasy Novella Series

Ella and the Elementals

Ella and the Multiverse

Ella and the Monsters

Ella and the Dreamers

Supernatural Short Stories

Dead Souls

Dead Souls II

The Shadow

Writing as A. S. French

Crime Fiction and Thrillers

The Astrid Snow series

Don't Fear the Reaper

The Killing Moon

Lost in America

Gone to Texas

The Final Girl

Snowstorm: An Astrid Snow Collection

The Ophelia Red series

Ophelia Red

The Detective Jen Flowers series

The Hashtag Killer

Serial Killer

Night Killer

The Killer Inside Them

The Frank Walker series

Where The Bodies Are Buried

Bodies of Evidence

Crime Short Stories

Crime Stories: A Collection

Call Me: An Astrid Snow Short Story

Go to www.andrewsfrench.com for more information.

The Dead Actress in the Painting

It's hard to be found when nobody knows you're lost.

Dianne Fox stood in front of the mirror and adjusted her hat and dark glasses.

If I don't get it just right, someone might recognise me.

She wore the same things whenever she went out, regardless of the time of year or whether it was during the day or night. Dianne couldn't admit it to herself, but it wouldn't make any difference what she wore: nobody had recognised her for over fifty years.

At least they hadn't recognised her as the person she used to be.

'Are you going to the car boot sale, Ms Fox?'

She turned from the mirror to answer Shelley. Shell, as she preferred, but Dianne could never sink that low, had only worked for Dianne for two weeks. Reliable cleaners were scarce nowadays, and she'd hired Shelley from a card in the window of the local newsagents. The agency she'd used before was so short of staff she thought they might have to close.

'Yes, Shelley.' She adjusted the glasses so they didn't

squeeze against her nose. 'As you get to know me, you'll realise how much I enjoy browsing for a bargain.'

Shelley's eyes filled with concern. 'Be careful on the racecourse car park. The ground is so uneven in some places. My friend Mary was only there for the races two weeks ago, and she got her heel stuck in a pothole and turned her ankle. It was a good job she'd supped a few glasses of fake champers beforehand, or the pain would have been unbearable. That's what she told me, anyway.' She laughed like a drunken hyena.

Dianne smiled as she checked there were enough pound coins in her purse for the boot sale. 'You'll make sure you lock the door when you leave?'

Shelley looked mortified. 'Of course, Ms Fox. This isn't my first rodeo, you know.'

The word rodeo made Dianne smile, thinking of the title track on her second album, *Rodeo Rodeo*.

If I burst into song now, singing rodeo rodeo, where did you go, would Shelley's face suddenly change with recognition? Would her eyes bulge wider than a frog when she understood she was working not for Dianne Fox, but Di Starr, Britain's new Marianne Faithfull, the singing sensation of 1970?

She glanced behind the cleaner, staring at the shelves full of porcelain figurines collected over the years. None of them had any monetary value, but they were worth something to her. Dianne put all the valuables upstairs, the jewellery and other gifts she'd kept from her brief, two-year brush with fame. These included the signed bracelet from Mick Jagger, the ring from David Bowie, plus the love letters and poems from Jim Morrison.

The thought of those and the time she spent with him in America in 1969 brought a smile to her face. She continued to think of the Lizard King as she replied to her cleaner.

'Okay, Shelley. Just do the upstairs today and I'll see you tomorrow morning for the rest.' She liked to have the cleaner come to the house two or three times a week. Not that Dianne made much mess, but she wanted the company.

Loneliness is a disease. And the only cure is other people.

But other people had let her down so many times she found trust a hard thing to find.

Just like fame, it was a fleeting thing that disappeared if you weren't paying attention.

She left the house with the sun on her face and the smell of fresh roses in the garden. Next door's black cat crossed her path and peered at her.

It's a good job I'm not superstitious, isn't it Fudge?

However, she was always adamant she'd endured more than her fair share of bad luck since signing that record contract in 1969.

Marianne had Andrew Loog Oldham, while I got Chuck Dante, the worst manager in the music business.

She pushed the memory of the horrible man from her mind as she crossed the road and set off on the thirty-minute trek to the racecourse. Dianne knew many of her neighbours would think it unwise for a woman of her age to walk the four-mile round trip unaccompanied, but she didn't care.

The journey helped her to select the correct memories from the carousel stored in her mind. Occasionally, one of the darker ones would intrude on her happy thoughts, but she accepted you could never appreciate the good things in life without undergoing the worst of its trials.

An image of Marianne Faithfull popped into her head

again, as it always did when she stumbled along the nostalgia path. Even though they moved in the same musical circles for that brief period, Dianne had only met her twice. Both were at parties where there was no time for proper introductions. Dante perceived the two women as rivals, which always made Dianne laugh.

I was never as pretty or talented as Marianne. Even when I went through my sex and drugs phase, I could never make it as interesting as her life.

But Dianne wasn't jealous. Such a thing was beyond her, knowing her fall from grace was a combination of bad luck and being surrounded by the wrong people.

Still, her life had got back on track by the end of the 1970s, and though she was never to sing again, she had some money left over to keep her on the straight and narrow. So even when those more obscure than she were discovered thirty and forty years later, her star – no pun intended – never resurfaced.

Her only piece of good luck was one of her old record labels sent her a check for royalties from sales in Japan going back to the seventies. Dante was long gone, she assumed, ironically, to a fiery pit full of demons poking him with sharp sticks. And that meant she could live out the twilight of her life with no money worries, buying things to brighten up her home.

Ten years ago, George, her neighbour, tried to show Dianne how to use the internet. She'd told him of her past, and he wanted to help.

'Get yourself a website, post some videos, tell some stories. Then, a new generation will discover the singing sensation Di Starr. You'll be famous again.'

She was reluctant, but George talked her into letting him do the internet stuff since she was clueless about it.

Even now, she didn't own a mobile phone because she didn't know how to use one.

So, after forty years of obscurity, she allowed herself to get excited about being Di Starr. Until her bad luck resurfaced with a killer blow: a hit-and-run driver knocked George over as he was on his way home from work.

Still, Dianne put on her hat and glasses and went to his funeral.

Now, as she strolled down the road, she glanced into the sky and noticed the weather was similar to the day they lay George into the ground.

Dianne got to the car boot sale an hour after the gates had opened. It meant she missed the mad rush of the initial crowd, which tended to be stressed looking women dragging small children with them, desperate loners hanging onto scruffy dogs, and middle-aged men with comb-overs and stomachs you could stand a chair on.

She paid her one-pound entrance fee to a sour-faced woman chewing gum and strode through the gates. For this once a week bargain extravaganza, about fifty per cent of the sellers would be regulars. Dianne only gave these a cursory glance unless they had something new. She always took a large plastic bag with her – even though she knew plastic bags were frowned upon by the modern world – but occasionally, she'd find a few things too large for her to carry. Sometimes she'd leave those behind with an ache in her heart, or if the sellers were willing, got them to deliver the item to her house.

That's how she'd bought the watercolour painting of Louise Brooks, which hung in her living room, as well as the 1930s book collection of detective mysteries.

So she was looking forward to this but was disappointed when she entered to see it was only about half full with sellers. And that surprised her. The excellent weather usually brought out the part-time sellers, and they had the stalls she liked to browse the most.

Dianne lowered her expectations as she started on the first row, avoiding the bunch of scruffy looking men with weather-beaten faces accompanied by rather hard-faced women standing in front of battered white vans. Instead, she spotted a table of what she called "family sellers" and headed for them.

These were often distinguished as a typical family group of mum, dad and a couple of small kids who might have been dragged along to lend a hand but rarely did.

She moved away from a large man stuffing a burger and fries into his mouth and stepped towards the box of jewellery. Her fingers glided over the items, her eyes attracted to the glitter, her skin enjoying the touch of the different designs and materials. Even when she bought nothing, like she wouldn't with this table, sometimes it would jog a happy memory from her mind. She put the rings and necklaces back, receiving a frown from the teenage girl all dressed in black behind the table. But it had reminded her of a steamy night shared with Marc Bolan and David Bowie.

A shiver ran down her spine as she moved between sellers, dipping in where she spotted something unusual or curious, moving on when it turned out to be a cheap replica or it was damaged.

Usually, she could spend a leisurely half an hour browsing the tables on a good buying day, but this afternoon she covered ninety per cent of it, spending no money.

There was only one table left to check, and her heart sank when she saw it stocked with videotapes, broken crockery, and what looked like twenty copies of *Fifty Shades of*

Grey. She was about to turn away when she noticed the sheet draped over something large near the seller.

The last dregs of customers were inching their way out of the boot sale when Dianne approached the bleary-eyed woman next to the mystery item.

'What's behind the cover?'

The woman grinned at her through nicotine-stained teeth.

'That's a painting my grandad had in his attic for years. I thought it might sell, but people kept moaning about it. So I covered it up.'

Dianne's curiosity antenna sprang into action. 'What were they complaining about?'

The seller shook her head. 'Potential buyers wouldn't approach the table because of the eyes.'

She moved to the side and removed the cover. Dianne stared at the canvas, seeing a woman peering back at her. She looked like she was in her mid-twenties, with a dark bob, wearing a black dress, sitting in a chair made from skulls. The dress was hitched onto her knees, revealing what Dianne thought were impressive legs.

But they weren't what caught her attention and what she assumed people were complaining about.

That was the eyes.

The more she peered at the painting, the more she felt the eyes staring straight at her. Even when she moved to the side, it was as if the eyes followed her. She guessed if you gazed at it for too long, it might be uncomfortable.

But Dianne was made of sterner stuff than the others. The gaze didn't worry her; it fascinated her. So she kept on looking at it as she spoke to the seller.

'Who is the subject?'

The woman shrugged. 'I don't know, love. My grandad

had it for maybe fifty years, and I don't know where he got it. The story I was told is when his first wife died, he stored the painting in the attic because his second wife, my gran, hated it.' She glanced at the frame behind her. 'It's the eyes, isn't it?'

Dianne ignored the question and replied with one of her own.

'How much do you want for it?'

The woman poked at her yellow teeth as the last of the customers drifted out of the boot sale. Dianne watched the movement in her face, knowing she was calculating how much she could get without blowing the sale.

'How about five pounds?'

Dianne smiled. 'I'll give you twenty if you deliver it to my home this afternoon.'

She saw the sparkle in the woman's eyes.

'Done,' she said as she stuck her hand out.

Dianne removed a pen and paper from her purse and wrote her address on it. Then she placed it into the woman's trembling fingers.

As she turned to leave, she had one last look at the painting, seeing the mystery woman's eyes watching her go.

* * *

She took the same route home, smiling as the sun caressed her face. Birds circled her, and music came from the houses on her right. Dianne didn't know what the song was – she hadn't kept up with popular music after her singing career collapsed – but it was a catchy tune that made her hum on the return journey.

Along the way, Dianne wondered who the person in the painting was and how she could find out. She knew she could discover the provenance of the frame and its subject using the internet, but she did not know how to do that.

Perhaps I could ask Shelley to do it.

Yes, that's what she'd do tomorrow.

The thought put a spring in her step, reminding her of that day over fifty years ago when she first stepped into the recording studio, and she sang as if her life depended on it.

* * *

The kettle had just boiled when the woman delivered the painting. She carried it into the house and placed it in the living room.

'Are you going to hang it in here?'

'I don't know yet,' Dianne said. 'I need to study it some more.'

The woman laughed. 'Don't put it in your bedroom. Those eyes won't let you sleep at night.'

Dianne gave her the twenty-pound note and ushered her out. Then she made her cup of tea and took it into the living room. The canvas was against the far wall, uncovered but with its back to her. She went to it and ran her fingers over the painting.

There was a lump under the brown paper. She reached into the top corner and peeled the paper away, finding a small envelope taped to the back of the canvas. Dianne removed it and took it with her tea to the sofa. She placed the cup on the table and stared at what was in her hand.

She did that for a minute before opening the envelope. Inside was a small card. She removed it and read the words printed on it.

'Emily Antonio. Actress.'

Dianne held it in her hands as the tea went cold.

Emily Antonio. Actress.

She sat like that for ten minutes. Then she got up and went to the painting. Dianne turned it around to look at it.

'Hello, Emily.'

Dianne smiled at what she'd purchased for such a small amount. Not only was it an enigmatic painting, now there was a mystery attached to it.

She gripped the side, deciding where to hang it, when she noticed something different about it.

The dress is lower on her legs.

That couldn't be right. She remembered it being higher when she'd admired those impressive pins. But the dress was unquestionably longer now.

Dianne moved closer to the painting, inspecting it in finer detail.

The skull chair was different as well. They appeared to be twisted more to peer away from the viewer.

Did the woman bring me a different copy?

She must have.

Dianne sighed before looking at the canvas again. It didn't matter. What she had was still a curiosity, and now she had a name to give to Shelley tomorrow.

She left the painting where it was and went upstairs for her afternoon nap. Later she would come down, cook some pasta, and decide where to hang the picture.

But she didn't.

* * *

She slept the rest of the day, waking at eight in the morning feeling as bad as she had for a long time. When she crawled out of bed and checked the time, there were only thirty minutes before Shelley arrived.

Dianne rubbed her cheek as she stumbled into the bathroom. Like every other morning, she ignored the mirror while throwing water over her face. Her mouth tasted as if something had died in it overnight. She squeezed toothpaste onto a brush and cleaned her teeth.

By the time she changed her clothes and made it downstairs, there were only ten minutes before the cleaner would arrive. She thought she'd be hungry but felt nothing, not even for a craving for her first cup of tea of the day.

She went to the living room and slumped onto the sofa. Shelley had a key to the house, so there was no need to let her in. A constant ache affected the whole of her body, but it was worse in her legs. Dianne reached down to scratch her knee when she glanced to look at the canvas: it wasn't where she'd left it.

A stitch erupted in her ribs as she clutched at her throat. Her knees creaked as she stood and looked around the room, a jolt hitting her heart as she saw the painting hanging on the wall above the fireplace.

Did I get up in the middle of the night and put it there?

She must have. It was the only answer.

God, my memory is getting worse by the day.

Dianne went towards it, feeling the vibration in her chest increase with every step. She stopped a few feet from it, peering at the dress to ensure it was the same as the last time she'd seen the painting.

It was, but something else had changed.

Her arms had moved. They were on Emily's knees now, resting there as her head tilted forward, staring directly at Dianne.

I must be imagining all of this. If I could forget about getting up in the night to hang this painting, I must be misremembering what the canvas was like.

She stepped closer, putting one hand on the fireplace as she scrutinised the image of Emily Antonio. Dianne couldn't take her gaze from the dead actress, feeling herself being pulled into the canvas.

'You bought a new painting.'

Dianne jerked backwards, with her fingers clutching onto the fireplace, the only thing stopping her from falling. Her heart rate doubled as she stared at the cleaner.

'I... I didn't hear you come in.'

Shelley rushed forward and grabbed her arm.

'Are you okay? You look exhausted.'

'Yes, I'm fine. Take me to the sofa. I need you to do me a favour.'

Shelley did as instructed, helping Dianne to sit down.

'Have you eaten Ms Fox?'

She brushed away the question with a wave of her wrinkled hand.

'I'll eat later. Do you have your little phone with you?'

Shelley narrowed her eyes. 'My mobile? I go nowhere without it. Isn't it about time you got one?'

Dianne patted the seat. 'Come, sit next to me. I need you to look for something on that magic web of yours.'

Shelley's laugh highlighted the many lines on her face. 'Sure, I'll search the internet for you.' She removed the phone from her pocket and tapped on the screen. 'What are you after?'

'Emily Antonio. She was an old movie actress. Will she be on your magic web?'

Shelley glanced at the canvas. 'Is that the woman in your new painting? I couldn't look at it for too long. There's something in her eyes that made the hairs stand up on the back of my neck. Doesn't it do the same for you?'

'No. Now can you find Emily for me?'

It took Shelley less than a minute to locate the information. She showed Dianne the phone.

'Can you read that, or do you want me to do it?'

Dianne took the phone and pulled it closer to her face. Then she read the details.

'Emily Antonio, 2 May 1908 – 16 September 1932, was a British stage and screen actress. She began her acting career in 1928, appearing in several Broadway productions. In addition, she appeared in minor roles in silent films, all of which are lost. Problems with her accent meant she couldn't make the transfer to the early talkies. Frustration with this led to her taking her own life outside Universal Studios in 1932.'

'A lot of young women got chewed up by the movie studios then,' Shelley said.

Dianne returned the phone to her. 'Is there anything else on there?'

Shelley flicked her finger across the screen, tutting as she went.

'There isn't much, but there is one interesting titbit.' She turned sideways so she couldn't see the painting. 'Emily didn't find fame in life, or death, like some others.'

'What do you mean?' Dianne said.

'Well, on the day Emily took her life, another struggling actress did the same thing, but in such a dramatic way she's remembered as "The Hollywood Sign Girl".'

Dianne nodded. 'I think I've heard of that. Didn't she jump from the top of the Hollywood sign in Beverly Hills?'

'Yes,' Shelley said. 'That was Peg Entwistle, a New York stage actress. She made the arduous hike up the canyon hill to the Hollywood Sign. She climbed fifty feet up a workman's ladder to the top of the "H" and plunged to her death. Her suicide filled the headlines in the Hollywood papers the next day, leaving Emily Antonio's death a footnote in the news.'

Dianne settled onto the sofa. 'How terrible.'

Shelley got up. 'Shall I clean the downstairs now?'

'Yes,' Dianne said. 'But you can leave this room as it is.'

The cleaner nodded, lowering her head as she left, so her face was away from the canvas.

Dianne turned to it, staring at the tragic woman who had taken her life so long ago.

When was the painting done, and why? Was there more to your suicide than a failed movie career?

She sat there and thought about those things, knowing she'd get up soon to make something to eat. But she wasn't hungry yet, relaxing her back into the sofa as Emily Antonio peered deep into her.

Shelley never mentioned how Emily had taken her life but said it was outside a movie studio. What was Emily's connection to that studio?

Dianne continued to stare at the dead actress in the painting. A persistent ache rumbled through her stomach, and she knew she'd have to move soon to get some breakfast. At her age, Dianne's appetite was like a tiny bird's, but she realised it wouldn't be good for her as she hadn't eaten since yesterday.

Yet the sofa was so comfortable she didn't want to move. Emily's gaze bore into her, and she suddenly lost that ache in her heart.

Yes, I'll stay here for a little longer.

Dianne heard Shelley whistling next door. The sound settled into her head as Emily Antonio looked deep into her.

* * *

Two hours later, Shelley woke her.

'Ms Fox, are you okay?'

Dianne's head jerked up, staring into the face of the cleaner.

'What... what time is it?'

'It's eleven, Ms Fox. I've finished, and I'm off now.'

She stood with her back to the painting. Dianne rubbed the sleep from her eyes, lifting as her body returned to life. A large pit of emptiness possessed her stomach, and her mouth felt like she'd eaten sandpaper.

Dianne reached out to Shelley.

'Don't go yet. I need you to look for something on your phone again.'

Shelley straightened her back, moving to the side so Dianne could see the edge of the frame of the painting.

'Of course I will, Ms Fox, but it might be easier just to get you a mobile.'

Dianne shook her head, but the cobwebs still gathered inside her mind.

'No. I'm far too old for that. Instead, I want you to search for another name for me.'

The cleaner had the phone ready in her hand. 'Fire away.'

For the first time since George, Dianne said the name to someone else.

'Di Starr. Look for Di Starr on your magic web.'

It didn't take Shelley long to find some information.

'There's not much, Ms Fox. Even less than that dead actress.'

'Tell me,' Dianne said.

'Well, she doesn't have a Wiki page.' Dianne didn't know what that was. 'And there are no photos or videos on any sites. All I found was a small paragraph on a 1960s music page: Di Starr, one of many obscure female singers, unleashed on the British public at the tail end of the sixties. Had no hits and never toured.'

Dianne bit into her top lip. 'That's not true. I was big in Japan and played concerts in the north of England and Scotland in the first few months of 1970. I remember the cold biting into me on stage.'

Shelley narrowed her eyes. 'Di Starr is you?'

Dianne sighed. 'She was me. I'm so obscure I'm not even worth a mention on the magic web.'

Shelley slipped the phone into her pocket. 'I can help you with that.'

She moved further to the side, and Dianne saw the whole of the picture. Even from the sofa, she knew it had changed again. Emily had shifted in the chair; her head turned away, so she wasn't looking out of the frame anymore. Now it appeared as if she was peering at something only she could see.

'How can you help me?'

Shelley sat next to her.

'I'll get you on all the social media sites, write a Wiki page, start a Facebook group. That sort of thing, you know?' Dianne didn't know, but she nodded anyway. 'It's a shame there are no photos or videos of you online. We'll need more than text to get people interested.' She pursed her lips and scrutinised Dianne. 'I suppose we could do some TikTok clips.'

'I've got some things you could use on the magic web,' Dianne said.

Shelley's eyes sparkled. 'What things?'

Dianne gazed at the painting as she spoke.

'Some mementoes from my singing career: jewellery, correspondence from famous pop stars, love letters from Jim

Morrison.'

Shelley gasped. 'Jim Morrison? From The Doors?'

The ache in Dianne's stomach increased. 'Yes. We had a brief but lovely relationship. He was a much-misunderstood man. The poetry he sent me is wonderful.'

'He sent you poetry? What about song lyrics? Did he send you any of those?'

'Yes, I think so.'

'That's great, Ms Fox. We'll be able to do something online with that, definitely.'

'You'll have to do it yourself. All that magic web stuff is beyond me.'

Shelley touched her hand, and Dianne shivered. She couldn't remember the last time anyone had touched her.

'Of course, Ms Fox.' She stood. 'This is going to be a fantastic adventure.' Dianne saw her glance at the painting, seemingly unaware it had changed. 'I have to go now. I've got another house to clean, but I'll come back tomorrow. Is that okay?'

Dianne nodded. 'Thank you for doing this. I don't know how to repay you.'

Shelley laughed. 'Think nothing of it. It will be exciting. But you make sure you have something to eat. I'll let myself out and see you tomorrow.'

Dianne smiled at her, wanting to get up but having no strength in her legs. Instead, she watched the cleaner leave and waited for the sound of the front door closing.

But she didn't hear it.

'She's gone straight upstairs to steal your valuables.'

Dianne turned her head to see where the voice had come from, but she already knew who it was. The canvas was empty, with no Emily or skull chair. The dead actress was out of the painting, sitting in the skulls opposite Dianne.

'Are you Emily Antonio?'

The woman smiled. 'You know who I am.' Those impossible eyes peered at the ceiling. 'Can't you hear her rumbling around in your bedroom?'

All Dianne could hear was the blood boiling in her veins and her heartbeat thumping in her ears.

'How is this possible?'

Emily uncrossed her legs, and the dress was above her knees again.

'I had a contract with Universal Studios. Do you know them?' Dianne nodded. 'They'd enjoyed hits in '31 with *Dracula* and *Frankenstein*. Horror films were popular with the public, and Universal had more success in 1932 with *Murders in the Rue Morgue, The Mummy* and *Island of Lost Souls.*

'They loved my British accent, believing I'd be a female Lugosi. So they offered me a contract for a role in what they hoped would be their next big horror smash. I would play an alluring vamp, catching men with my beauty before draining their blood. The painting was part of the publicity, but the film never got made, and the studio cancelled my contract. I protested, but they didn't care. So I did the only thing left to me.'

'You took your own life outside the studio gates.'

Emily sighed, and the temperature dropped in the room. 'And look where it got me. It was my protest against the way I'd been used, how different powerful men had promised me things if I gave them what they wanted in return.' Her eyes sank into Dianne's. 'You know what I mean, don't you, Di?'

Dianne tried to think of the recording studio, but all she remembered was what she'd been forced to do to get there.

Her lips trembled. 'Yes.'

Emily Antonio looked at the empty painting. 'I don't know how my soul ended up inside that frame, but it wasn't long before I was shut away for years.' Dianne's skin crawled when the dead actress laughed. 'First, they abuse us, and then they lock us up. Hasn't it always been the way?'

Dianne tried to stop her hands from shaking. 'I have a good life now.'

Emily's shoulders trembled as her laughter made the skulls rattle in the chair.

'No, you don't, Di. You have a life of staggering boredom. You try to fill it with trivial things while all the time denying what they did to you.'

'That's going to change. Finally, people will know who I am; they'll know who I was.'

Emily Antonio shook her head. 'No, they won't, Di. Your domestic help will take all of your valuables for herself. She'll put the Lizard King's poetry and lyrics on the internet and claim it as her own. Shelley will sell all your jewellery, and you'll never see her again after today.' She pointed at the ceiling. 'Can't you hear her up there stealing your life from you?'

Something dropped to the floor upstairs, and Dianne jumped. The fire crept over her brain while ice ran over her skin.

'What can I do?'

Emily leant out of the chair, with the flesh peeling away from her face.

'You know what you have to do. Don't make the same mistake I did. You can't get back what was taken from you, but you'll be remembered forever if you go one step further than I did.'

Dianne stood. As she did, she glanced at the top of Emily's head, seeing the worms wriggling inside her hair. Her legs trembled as she moved to the door and stepped out of the living room. She put her hand on the bannister and walked upstairs like a tortoise.

But only yesterday, she'd seen a clip on the news of a tortoise killing and eating a bird.

When she got to the top, she heard the noise in her bedroom.

'Shelley, are you in there?'

The sound stopped, and the cleaner came out of the room. She held a necklace and envelopes in her fingers.

'You shouldn't have come up here, Ms Fox.'

Dianne gripped onto the bannister. 'What are you going to do?'

Shelley grinned at her. 'What I have to. I'm not going back to prison for an old bat like you.'

Her hands were open as she lunged for Dianne. She dropped the jewellery to the floor and stood on it. That's when she turned her ankle and fell towards the top of the stairs. Dianne was pressed against the wall, so the cleaner missed her when she tried to grab Dianne's leg.

Shelley fell into the first step and then kept on falling, tumbling until she hit bottom. The crack of the broken neck hurt Dianne's ears.

She stood there for two minutes, unsure what to do until she heard Emily's voice.

'Come and see me one last time, Dianne.'

The ache had disappeared from her legs as she went downstairs and into the room. She stared at the dead actress.

'It was an accident.'

Emily smiled. 'Of course, it was. Nobody would ever think an old woman could do that. But you still know what you have to do, don't you?'

Dianne did.

The pain had vanished from the whole of her as she returned upstairs. She got to the top as Dianne Fox, but she was Di Starr again when she reached the bottom. She took the love letters into the living room and gazed at Emily Antonio in the painting.

Then she went one step further.

* * *

The police kicked in the door two days later. If Shelley Clark's parole officer hadn't informed them she was not returning his calls, they might not have got there for weeks or months. Instead, they checked through her client list until arriving at Dianne Fox's house and looking through the glass on the front door to see the body at the bottom of the stairs.

Detective Inspector Lee Allen and Detective Constable Suzanne Bignell watched their colleagues from Forensics at work.

'The cleaner had her throat cut using the knife the house owner used on herself,' DI Allen said.

They went into the living room. Letters and envelopes had been placed around the body in the shape of a heart.

'So, it's a murder-suicide crime scene,' DC Bignell said.

'It looks like it,' Allen replied. 'I guess it will make more sensational headlines than just a suicide. People will never forget this.'

One of the Forensic team held a piece of paper in his hand.

'These are love letters.'

DI Allen narrowed his eyes at the body on the carpet.

'There's a bit of an age gap between the two of them.'

The Forensic Officer shook his head.

'No, these letters are from Jim Morrison.'

'Wow,' DC Bignell said.

DI Allen turned away from the body and looked at the painting on the wall. He moved closer to it, convinced he recognised the young woman in the canvas. She was standing inside a recording studio with her face pressed against a microphone.

She was beautiful, and he would have sworn she was looking straight at him.

'People are strange,' he said as he imagined what her singing voice was like.

Hauntology

I was about to give up and call it a day when the old woman smashed a bust of Britney Spears over a skinny man's head. Bits of porcelain flew everywhere, missing my nose by inches as they bounced off the wall and fell into the bowls shaped like bare-breasted mermaids near my feet. It wasn't the start of the seaside holiday I'd expected.

My heart thumped against my ribs as I rushed to the stricken man, only to find it was a showroom dummy with the face of David Beckham.

'I've always hated that thing,' the woman said. 'My ex-husband bought it for me as a birthday present one year.' Her eyes sparkled like shooting stars. 'Can you imagine that?'

I was unsure if she was talking about the bust or the mannequin. I picked Britney's eye from my clothes and offered it to her. 'Wasn't it worth money?'

She laughed through nicotine-stained teeth, moving close enough for me to smell the lavender in her hair. 'The locals, who all hate me, by the way, like to think of this place as an antique shop, but it's all just junk.' She grabbed the eye from me. 'I haven't seen you in here before. Are you a tourist?'

I nodded. 'I'm renting the cottage on the cliff. I needed privacy for my work.'

The woman stuck a withered finger into her mouth and retrieved something that might have been meat once. Then she ate it as she spoke.

'What work would that be, love? Are you a parapsychologist?'

'Oh no,' I said. 'I'm not brave enough to jump out of a plane.'

She narrowed her eye at me before grabbing her side and laughing. 'That's a good one.' She thrust a hand out. 'I'm Judy, owner of this house of junk.'

I gripped her hand, which was stronger than she looked. 'I'm Emily, a music researcher and part-time DJ.'

Judy nodded. 'One of those noisy people, eh? What are you researching for – a book?'

'Yes. My dad used to tell me this area had an underground music scene in the late 70s that nobody has written about, so I thought I'd look around and take a vacation by the sea at the same time.'

'Well, I don't know about that,' Judy said. 'Music gives me a headache, but there's a pile of records at the back of the shop if you want to have a gander. Or do you youngsters not bother with that stuff now because you're all obsessed with the internet and music in the clouds?'

I smiled at her. 'Not all of us.' I glanced over my shoulder. 'At the back, you said?'

'Aye, you look while I put the kettle on. I might have some chocolate biscuits the cat hasn't eaten.'

Judy shuffled off as I moved between the narrow shelves, standing on David Beckham's head as I did. His nose crunched under my shoe as I surveyed the surroundings. The junk shop was a cramped and dusty space, with stacks of cardboard boxes and towering shelves of knick-knacks and bric-à-brac. The air was musty and thick, and the smell of burnt wood and paper mingled with the scent of dirt and rusty metal. I tasted grit and dust around me, coating my tongue and tickling my throat. The shelves were overflowing with an eclectic mix of old books, vintage cameras, tarnished silverware, and countless trinkets of indeterminate origin. Peeling wallpaper covered the walls, and the floorboards creaked with each step.

The lighting was dim, with flickering fluorescent bulbs casting strange shadows on the shelves and walls. I squinted, trying to make out the details of each item, but the shadows danced and twisted, obscuring my surroundings. The only bright spot in the place was a shaft of sunlight streaming through a dusty window, illuminating a small corner of the shop.

As I reached the back, I spotted old vinyl records perched on a shelf in the corner. The covers were grimy and faded, with peeling edges and frayed corners. I sifted through the stack, hoping to find something interesting, but discovering stuff I'd seen many times before: the Sex Pistols record with a Sid Vicious doll in a coffin, The Faith Tones album *Jesus Use Me*, a naked Roy Harper, and Mötley Crüe's greatest hits, which must have been a silent album.

There was a lot more trash to go through, but at the bottom was something I'd never seen before – the image on the cover was the face of a woman with sewn-up lips and dark shadows around the eyes, like a Mexican death mask. The band's name, Hauntology, was scrawled in bold letters across the top. Or maybe that was the title, as there was no other text. The faded art and the worn edges of the sleeve gave it an air of mystery that I couldn't resist.

I Googled the name but only got a link to a series of articles about the word's meaning. There was no information about a band or album title with that name. I even took a photo of the cover, tried an image search, and got nothing.

The sound of the kettle boiling sparked me into life, and I returned to the front of the shop with my treasure.

'I only have green tea,' Judy said. 'Is that okay?'

'Sure.' I showed her the album. 'Do you know anything about this?'

Judy pushed the glasses up on her nose and peered at the record. 'Yes – it's called Hauntology and has a scary woman on the cover.'

'I think it's some Mexican death makeup. You don't remember where this came from?'

She shook her head. 'I inherited the shop when my sister died. So I don't know what half the stuff in here is or its worth. And I don't care.'

I sipped at the tea, and it warmed my lips. I removed the vinyl from the cover, disappointed to find it in a plain inner sleeve. The label was empty, with no mention of the artist or who produced it. So I examined the black marble. Practically since day one, the inside track or run-out groove of a vinyl record or 78rpm disc had been the domain of the matrix number, an alphanumerical code either stamped or handwritten into the wax to help pressing plants assign the correct stamper and label to each side of the record. Extra digits often referred to the cut or take of a particular record, while some plants or cutting engineers assigned their own signatures to the space. Far from an exact science, collectors often considered matrix numbers as proof of first pressings or sought-after alternate takes and re-cuts. All this code was rather formal in contrast to the hidden messages that had since jostled for space alongside their more conventional brethren in the run-out groove.

The legendary mastering engineer George Peckham was the chief architect of messages etched into vinyl records. He signed off many of the hundreds of thousands of records he cut from the '60s onwards with his nickname "Porky" or "A Porky Prime Cut". Occasionally he'd respond to lyrics on the record with witty asides. On others, like Elvis Costello's 1978 album, *This Year's Model*, he'd kick-start frenzied competitions by inscribing telephone numbers that fans could call to win prizes. While Led Zeppelin's 'Immigrant Song' 7" carried the words "Do What Thou Wilt Shall Be The Whole Of The Law", a quote from so-called occultist Aleister Crowley. Every piece of vinyl I'd ever owned had something scratched into the run-out groove – but not this one.

'You don't know this band, Hauntology?' I said.

Judy broke a chocolate biscuit in two and dropped half into her green tea.

'My dear, the last time I listened to music, Elvis was still in the army.'

I rechecked the back of the album cover, a collage of tiny images, peering at grinning skulls with no text anywhere.

'What do I owe you for it, Judy?' I reached into my pocket and removed a twenty-pound note.

'Keep your money. I'm glad to get rid of the thing – that woman's face gives me the heebie-jeebies.'

I finished the tea and thanked her, desperate to return to the cottage to listen to the album and thankful I'd brought my portable turntable and speakers. The heavens broke as I left the shop, forcing me to thrust the record under my top and pull my jacket close to me. I ran over cobbled streets, dodging excitable dogs and stray children before reaching my holiday home just as lightning cracked open the clouds.

I removed the vinyl and scrutinised it in more detail, astonished to see no scratches or marks. The cover design gave it an early 1980s look, but perhaps it was something recent where the artist or the designer had opted for a retro style. I set up the turntable and carefully placed the record on it. A woman's voice slithered from the black marble as soon as the needle hit the groove, a lilting, delicate tone that transported me to an unknown time and place. The music that filled the room was hauntingly beautiful, with a retro-futuristic sound that felt both of its time and ahead of it. It was like nothing I had ever heard before. The world faded away as I became lost in the sounds. It was as if the band was playing just for me, their notes and melodies weaving a spell around me. I closed my eyes and let the sonic waves wash over me, losing myself in its beauty and her ethereal voice.

However, as the record played on, I felt a strange sense of unease. It was like someone was watching me, a creeping sensation I wasn't alone. I tried to ignore it, but it only grew stronger as the music continued. I opened my eyes and looked around the cottage, but everything was as it should have been. The windows were closed, and the door was locked. Even so, I couldn't shake the feeling something else was with me as I immersed myself in the first side of the vinyl.

The time passed in a blur, and I wasn't sure how long it had lasted as the needle reached the end and lifted off the vinyl to return to its resting place. I got up and turned the record over, eager to hear side two. This time, I paid atten-tion to each note, sound, and every whisper. It was as if the band was trying to communicate with me through the music, telling me a beautiful and tragic story that I couldn't fully understand because the lyrics were impossible to decipher.

As the night wore on, I became obsessed with this mysterious group and their female singer. So I searched online again for information about them but got the same results. I visited numerous music forums, posted questions, and uploaded the cover, but nobody knew anything about Hauntology or the record. Several people thought it might be a hoax or a musical version of Banksy, with some famous musicians releasing it as a joke. I tried recording the album to my phone to upload the tracks online, but the sound came out distorted and twisted, so I didn't bother.

Only when my stomach rumbled did I realise I'd been listening to the music for hours and had eaten nothing. So I left it playing behind me and went to the fridge, retrieving what remained of the previous night's Indian takeaway. I warmed it up in the microwave and returned to the main room with the food and a bottle of wine.

As I ate and drank, I focused on the woman's voice, attempting to decipher the lyrics, but it proved impossible – whoever the singer was, Hauntology were like a cross between the Cocteau Twins and Dead Can Dance. Either she was singing in a constructed language or it was so obscure I couldn't decipher the words.

The music continued to play as I fell asleep on the sofa.

I don't know how long I slept, but the record was still playing when I woke. Somehow, the needle arm must have got stuck in a loop instead of returning to its cradle after the side had finished. My arms and neck ached as I stood, needing the toilet but stopping before I put one foot forward: the music had altered. And so had her lyrics. Now, there were words I understood; not all, but enough: flight, sacrifice, love, honour, desperation, and descent.

My legs trembled as I stumbled towards the record player, thinking somebody had broken into the cottage and changed the vinyl for something else. Someone was playing a practical joke on me; that had to be it.

Then I heard a noise that sent chills down my spine. It was a whisper, so faint I almost missed it. But as I listened closer, it was the singer calling my name.

'Emily.'

I froze in front of the turntable. 'Who's there?'

There was no answer. I was alone, with only the record and my thoughts for company.

I was hearing things again. Movement returned to my legs, and I went to the bedroom and grabbed my bag, opening it to find the pills still there. I stared at them for a minute, ready to fall back to the crutch that had supported me for six months before tossing them on the bed.

Then I went to the living room, used the last of the wine to fill my glass, and slumped onto the sofa. As I sat there, I realised I had become consumed by my obsession with the music and Hauntology, so much I was hearing things that weren't there – like those Beatles songs that, if you played them backwards, were supposedly spells calling for the devil.

My ready-to-burst bladder shouted at me to go to the toilet, so I got up, snatching the needle from the record in mid-flow and turning the turntable off. Too much music was messing with my head. It wasn't the first time it had happened – I'd once spent an entire weekend listening to Primal Scream's *Screamadelica*, convinced that Bobby Gillespie was secretly in love with me.

The toilet seat was cold against my flesh as I put my face in my hands. Then a great idea struck me – I could use the Hauntology album in my next DJ set, mixing it with more modern dance music to see its effect on the audience. And perhaps that would shake the tree loose so somebody would come forward about the band.

I finished and washed my hands, peering at my reflection in the mirror as I mouthed the words all my old friends had taunted me with.

'You're only a DJ, not a proper musician.'

I'd tried to ignore the accusation, but it was always with me because I agreed with them. Even though I'd tried writing lyrics and taken guitar lessons, I knew I wasn't musical in any shape or form apart from spinning bits of vinyl in front of people. I could never be as good as whoever played and sang on the Hauntology album.

I smashed my fist into the wall, cracking the plaster and drawing blood from my knuckles. The pain stung my flesh and ran up my arm, taking a route in my head where familiar voices whispered to me.

'You'll always be a failure,' my father said.

'You have no talent,' my teachers said.

'You sing like a horse,' all my boyfriends said.

Again and again, the words pounded into my skull. I threw water over my face before returning to the living room, staring at the turntable. Whoever the artists were on that album, they'd been more creative than I ever would.

I went to the record player, turned it on and dropped the needle onto the first track. Having already listened to it over a dozen times, I knew what to expect, waiting for those ethereal female tones to spring forward before the guitars and drums joined it.

But there was nothing this time.

Only silence.

Silence, apart from the sound of the stylus scraping into the vinyl, and the noise of my heart thumping inside my head.

Then something else.

The voice.

The woman from Hauntology, but not singing – talking. Speaking to me.

'Hello, Emily.'

I stumbled, my legs giving way as I fell against the table, knocking the books to the carpet. Dust drifted into the air and assaulted my senses.

'Who said that?'

'Come closer, Emily.'

My feet moved without me telling them to, striding to the record as it circled the turntable.

'How is this possible?'

'Close your eyes,' she said.

So I did. 'Who are you?'

'I'm Sarah. Now open up, Emily.'

My eyelids flickered, struggling to adjust to the lights. I wasn't in the cottage anymore, standing in what looked like a recording studio. Cigarette smoke drifted through the air that smelled of stale beer and pizza.

I peered at the green-eyed woman with the blazing red hair. 'Where am I?'

Sarah pointed through the misted glass near me. 'That's Danny, the drummer. Next to him on guitars is Jamie, and we have Bianca on keyboards.'

Dry ice appeared at the back of my throat. 'How did I get here?'

'That doesn't matter. What's important is if you want to stay.'

'What do you mean?'

She touched my arm and a shiver ran through my flesh, before she turned me towards that emerald gaze. 'I'm retiring, Emily, so we need a replacement singer. That could be you if you want.'

I trembled in her touch. 'Are you Hauntology?'

'What?'

'That was the only word on the cover I found. Was that your album?'

She let go of me. 'No, we're recording the album now. All we require is your vocals.'

'Me? I can't sing.'

'Yes, you can, Emily. Close your eyes again.'

I did. 'I don't understand any of this. It must be a dream.'

'It's no dream, Emily. Now open up.'

The noise greeted me as I opened my eyes, staring at the thousands of people gazing at the band and me on the stage.

I pressed my hand into my chest. 'Wow!'

'This could be your future, Emily. If you want it.'

The crowd was shouting something, but I couldn't understand the words.

'I want it.'

'Good,' Sarah said before she put her hands over my eyes.

I didn't panic, smelling the aroma of fresh strawberries on her skin. 'What's happening?'

Sarah removed her hands, and we sat at a table in a large room. In front of me were paper and a pen.

'All you have to do is sign that contract, Emily, and everything you've ever wanted will come true.'

'What about you?' I said.

Her green eyes sparkled. 'Me? I'll join my friends Janis

and Jimi, sipping wine with Ami and Karen. It's your turn now.'

I took a deep breath and hesitated, my fingers trembling as they hovered over the pen.

Then I grabbed it.

It was another two weeks before the cottage owner entered his property. No one reported Emily missing because she had nobody who cared. Finally, the owner removed her things, thinking she'd left them behind when the rental finished, all but the record player and the album. He moved around them as if they weren't there.

Two months later, a failing economy forced the owner to list the property for sale, which stayed unsold for the rest of the year.

Then, early in the New Year, a newly married young couple moved into the cottage. They spent a week cleaning and rearranging before they found the record player and the album. Initially, they were confused about how it worked, since they only listened to music on their mobile phones.

But once they did, the man turned the player on and placed the needle on the vinyl.

And Emily sang.

The Resurrection will not be Televised

Don't call them zombies. Or dead heads.

The correct term for the returnees is the Born Again. I couldn't forget that, or it would be another failed interview. And this would be the worst. I had one day left of my unemployment credits, and I was out of reviews. No job equalled no money, which meant getting kicked out of my flat. Then I'd be homeless.

And I couldn't live like that again. I'd once spent six months sleeping on buses until the company caught on to what I was doing. In a city as large as this, the late-night busses that ran from midnight to seven in the morning were a godsend to people like me. All I had to do was find a quiet spot at the back, then snuggle up under a seat. It was perfect in the winter as the heat from the engine wiped the chill from the bones.

The day they threw me off was lucky in one way: two hours later, that bus went off the bridge and into the river.

I tried not to think of that as I headed for my interview. One of several positives that came out of the resurrection was the creation of new jobs. So I was determined not to waste this opportunity. I gazed over the city, raising my eyes above the grey buildings to the horizon, looking across the people scurrying back and forth, wondering if I'd find my worth in the world. The last time I'd seen my mother, she'd let rip with her usual rant, pointing out that a man was nothing without a job or a car. Or at least somewhere to live that wasn't a bed in a doss house.

So I'd dusted myself down and found a place to live using my meagre savings. I'd even had a couple of dates, but they'd come to nothing.

'Your father worked all his life,' my mother had shouted at me as I left. Her breath had burnt the back of my neck, its smell reminiscent of the chemicals lingering over my head as I strode through an industrial district.

I glanced at the steel giants as they coughed out smoke, finding it curious that a lot of the Born Again had been shifted away from the living and placed behind industry most people avoided. It took me half an hour to get there, striding through a junkyard of cars and into the building.

Nobody greeted me as I entered. The clock on the wall said five minutes to nine. This was an early start for me. The room was empty apart from a dozen vacant chairs and flowers stacked along the side: a mixed aroma of lilies, roses, and bluebells wafted around the chamber. It hadn't taken long for this former funeral parlour to transform itself into a resurrection company.

The Risen Corporation

The signs covered most of the walls, with no space for religious icons or mementoes. Most of the planet still wondered if this miracle came from science or God, so the Risen Corporation, like others, wouldn't commit themselves until one of the Born Again brought a definitive answer back with them.

That was one of many problems the resurrection had caused. None spoke about where they'd been. So there were no secrets of the afterlife, no revelations about God, and no descriptions of Heaven, Hell, or anywhere else. Not yet, anyway.

My mother used to tell me there are all kinds of dying, but only one way of being dead.

But that was over now.

People were desperate to learn from the resurrected, wanting to know if Hell existed. I sat there, waiting for my interview and thought of that question. I remembered those bus rides, of living on mouldy food and dirty water and of my mother's fire and brimstone and knew the answer to that question.

I wondered if my mother would be happy for me now or if she'd scold me for taking this type of work. I'd never known my father – he'd taken two in the chest in some long-forgotten war – so my mother never had it easy bringing me up.

'You need a work ethic, son,' she'd say as if it was something you could get in a shop or win on the lottery.

I never thought much of it then. There were all kinds of jobs when my father was alive. On our street, there was a woman who gave haircuts to dogs and a bloke who delivered manure to your doorstep. One of our neighbours would even go to your house and rearrange the furniture, so it aligned with the rhythm of your heart.

The smile crept across my face as I guessed such a thing wouldn't work with the Born Again.

I puffed out my cheeks and watched the hand on the clock turn to nine. The interviews started at ten, but I'd wanted to arrive before the others. I closed my eyes and went through the questions in my head again, trying to guess what they'd ask. My brain considered so many possibilities I didn't hear her sit next to me.

'The early bird catches the worm.'

The voice was unexpected and low. I opened my eyes to see her, perhaps a few years younger than me, in her mid-twenties, emerald eyes sparkling above delicate cheeks and purple lips. She had the biggest, most beautiful afro I'd ever seen, with a face to launch a thousand ships and a body to sink your soul.

'Wh... wh... what?' I'd gained a stutter previously unknown to me.

She crossed her legs and smiled. Her pinstripe suit appeared brighter and cleaner than mine. 'I hate being late for anything.' She glanced around the room. 'At least we beat the throng.'

It wasn't so much that you listened to her voice but bathed in it as it washed over you.

I pulled at my tie and spluttered. 'You think there'll be many applicants?'

She removed a nail file from her jacket and rubbed it across her nails. 'There are few proper jobs left for humans, not with those everywhere.' She stopped filing for a second and pointed at the tiny robot scuttling over the floor and picking up the dust.

I failed to control myself and cringed in disgust. How had I not seen it when I came in? My arm twitched and brushed against her leg.

'I'm sorry,' I said, making it worse by waving my fingers in the air and catching her again.

'Are you scared of robots?' Concern seeped from her, the remains of my heart melting further.

'No, no, not really.' I shut down the childhood memories

and focused on her face. I'd met no one with green eyes before.

She put the nail file away and brushed a piece of dust from her sleeve. 'It's those new androids I can't stand. But, of course, the automaton revolution was before my time, and it's great that people don't have to do all those back-breaking, dangerous jobs anymore, but a girl's got to live, you know?'

I nodded, but I didn't know. I hadn't had a girlfriend or female companion since Doris left me five years ago. 'You're here for the job, then?'

She looked at me as if I was stupid. I couldn't argue with that. 'My name is Lolly Zagadoo.' She held her hand out to me. My fingers trembled as I took hers in mine. Her flesh was cold to the touch.

'I'm Bob,' I said.

Lolly let go of me. 'Just Bob?'

I struggled to recall my surname. She ran a finger through her magnificent hair and waited for me to remember myself. My mind wilted inside my brain. 'It says Robert Johnson on my birth certificate.' I did my best to muster up a smile, desperate to clutch at my chest and tear out my beating heart. Her face lit up like a blazing sky on a summer's day.

'That's a splendid name; you've got lots of history behind you with that.'

'Thanks, Lolly.' Her name sounded fabulous when said out loud.

She settled into her chair and moved closer to me. 'We're competing for the same job, but there's no need for animosity. Have you done your homework for the interview?'

Homework was one of the few things I was good at, at

school. It helped me avoid my mother, so I had an excuse to hide in my bedroom.

'It's straightforward: the Risen Corporation requires a Welcomer for an immediate start. The salary is entry level. There are no other benefits.'

Lolly threw her hands in the air. 'There's a benefit apart from the money. We welcome the Born Again from their deathly sleep. It's a privilege to guide the poor, confused souls into their second lives.'

My feet twitched inside my shoes. There was a foreign object in my socks, and it irritated my toes. 'All we're supposed to do is record their names, cause of death, and ensure they adjust to their new surroundings quickly and smoothly.'

Her eyes sparkled. 'And if one of them babbles about what they experienced after death, what do we do then?'

I knew this bit by heart, having spent most of the night memorising the booklet the Risen Corporation had given me. 'We inform our Line Manager immediately.'

She squashed her lips together and shook her head. 'While doing that, what if the Born Again forget everything they learnt during the afterlife? Imagine the most important secret in human history lost because we have to notify some functionary.'

Her words surprised me. If she spoke like this in the interview, she'd have no chance of the job. Then a strange idea came crashing through my skull.

Was this all a test? Could it be part of the interview?

It scared and thrilled me to peer at her. 'We're not quali-fied to deal with the consequences.'

Lolly threw her arms in the air and sprang from the chair. 'Who is? The resurrection is new for everyone.'

She didn't wait for an answer, striding across the room

to the table where the Risen Corporation had provided fresh water and sandwiches for the applicants. She looked at the food and grimaced before turning to me.

'What would you do?' I said.

Lolly picked up a glass of orange juice and held it to her nose. Her fingers trembled as she put it back. 'It all depends on where we perceive ourselves in the great conundrum.'

I stared at her, scrutinising every inch of her face. This must be a test. She looked magnificent in that suit and a clean white shirt buttoned up to the top of her throat. I sweltered in the room, yet she stayed calm. Her hand had been refreshing to touch. A sudden thought struck me: maybe she was an android, sent here to question me about the Born Again.

'What is the great conundrum?' I felt the job slipping from me, which meant my life tumbled downhill and out of control.

Behind her head, the Risen Corporation sign shimmered. 'The resurrection changed the planet. It didn't matter about your previous beliefs. Once the first of the dead rose, your entire world shattered. But, six months later, everything revolves around the answer to the great conundrum: what will the living do with the returnees?'

Her words fascinated me, but I was no clearer in my understanding. I longed for a formal interview? 'And what's the answer?'

Lolly grabbed a spoon from the table and spun it through her fingers like a magician. 'In this modern world, where the resurrected and robots outnumber the living, we have to decide our relationship with those no longer dead.' She paused but continued to manipulate the cutlery. 'Now, we have Keepers and Quitters; do you know who they are?'

I nodded. 'Keepers believe the Born Again should be

integrated into society; Quitters argue they don't belong here and should be placed on an island somewhere, maybe dumped into the Australian outback. Extremist Quitters want the returnees dead again.'

'That's true, and now all of us find ourselves in one of those camps; there is no middle ground. But inside those two camps are various diverse factions; we have science versus religion, the possessed against the disposed, rich challenging the poor, privilege battling protest, and so on.'

I wondered at what point she'd ask me to take sides. I was now of the firm belief that Lolly Zagadoo wasn't here for a job interview. 'The Born Again present tough challenges for us all.'

'Do you remember the first day of the resurrection?'

I stuffed my hands into my pockets and pushed the jacket close to my legs. 'Who wouldn't?'

Her eyes lit up. 'Wasn't it exciting?'

The itch in my foot disappeared, and I laughed. 'That's one way of putting it. I was at the hospital.'

She took a stride towards me. 'You were ill?'

'No, just visiting a friend.' I lied. 'Then the screaming started. I ran out straight into a startled nurse. She pointed into the next room. I stepped inside to find a doctor shaking against a wall and an old woman sitting bolt upright on the bed. She'd died twenty minutes earlier.'

'Perhaps it was a misdiagnosis.'

'I assumed that until the howling came from the floor below.'

'You were above the morgue.'

She was correct. 'Over two dozen returnees were there. Pandemonium spread through the hospital.'

'And the world; at least we weren't in one of the more dangerous parts.'

'What do you mean?'

'We might have been living someplace where everyone has a gun.'

I knew what she meant. 'Some people thought it was the start of the zombie apocalypse and shot every returnee they found.' I'd watched the news clips of such events.

Lolly shook her head. 'Imagine returning from death, then to die once more because of the fear. And then some ignored the cries from the cemeteries, leaving Born Again to suffocate and suffer clasping at their coffins. And the dead wouldn't get a third chance.'

They were terrible images, many of them splashed across the internet.

'At least we got places like this.' I pointed at the sign for the Risen Corporation. 'Governments decided all those buried would be dug up and stored ready for their resurrection. And we can welcome them back.'

She grinned at me. 'It sounds as if you have the corporate line memorised to a tee. So, if a returnee asks you how life has changed since they died, what will you tell them?'

I crossed my arms and then uncrossed them, digging deep into my head for the answers I'd spent all night practising. 'Focus on the positives.'

'And what are those?'

The itch returned to my foot, and I did my best to ignore it. 'Well, it seems the Born Again return in better shape than when they left; any injuries or illnesses they had are gone. Studies of cells, blood samples, and DNA have so far shown that returnees don't age. They don't need to eat or drink. Their minds are fresh and uncluttered; any instances of dementia or Alzheimer's have disappeared.'

Lolly came over and sat next to me again. 'Are there any negatives?'

Might this be a trick? I ignored the sparkle in her eyes, but I couldn't overlook the itch which had travelled up my foot and infested my thigh. I scratched at it and contemplated her question. 'There are challenges they must overcome.'

'We all have those.' Her leg pressed into mine. A chill invaded my flesh. 'What trials will they face?'

I stuck out my chest and puffed out my cheeks. 'The returnees are dispossessed; everything they had in their previous life, money, property, possessions, went to any family they had, or to the State. Even if they still have a family and friends who agree to look after them, the law requires them to live in a State shelter for the first three months of their return.'

'Why is that?'

Now, I didn't doubt this was an interview. I wondered if Lolly Zagadoo would be my boss at the Risen Corporation if I got the job. The thought inflamed my cheeks, yet it remained cold in the room.

'Three-month close observation by State officials is for the welfare of the Born Again, to ensure they don't suffer physical or mental withdrawal symptoms or adverse effects to their new environment. But, of course, well....'

I didn't finish that thought.

'Well, what?'

Her fingers touched my knee. I couldn't move them, my lungs inhaling a blast of her jasmine perfume, and focused on the question. 'There are several conspiracy theories regarding the Born Again, claiming some have returned with knowledge of an afterlife. And many others want that information.'

Lolly removed her hand and stood. In my heart, it felt as if I'd been with her for hours. Yet the clock said fifteen minutes past nine. 'Can you name anything else the returnees have lost in their second chance at life?'

The red mist crept over my face again. 'Well, as far as anyone knows, after six months, none of them have shown any desire for, well, desire.'

Her laugh was loud and infectious. 'That could be positive and negative.'

It wasn't amusing to me. I peered at the Risen Corporation signs plastered over the walls. I thought getting a second chance at life was beautiful and miraculous. Whether that miracle was scientific or by Divine intervention didn't matter. But it couldn't be easy to be dispossessed and living in a government lodging, with no craving for food or sex.

I peered at her as she continued to laugh. 'I understand why some returnees take their own lives if they have no more desire.'

'Can't we exist without it?'

Lightbulbs blinked inside my head. 'Human existence is sparked by longing; food and drink, shelter and warmth, love and desire, a sense of purpose through work. These appear lost to the Born Again.'

'Then the world has to provide something meaningful for them, something worth living for.'

'And how do we do that?'

She sat next to me once more, taking my hand in hers. 'We start by making them realise what it is to be human again; we help them appreciate that, even with what they've lost, they can still find a connection with what surrounds them.' Lolly peered deep into my face. 'Do you understand?'

'This isn't an interview, is it?'

'No.'

'There isn't a job with the Risen Corporation?'

'No, there isn't.'

She had warm hands, but mine were cold. Her eyes were luminous, that magnificent hair wondrous, her beauty intoxicating, her intelligence enviable, and her charm joyous. But I felt no desire for her.

'Did I pass the test?'

She pressed her face into mine and then pulled away. 'Welcome to your new life, Robert Johnson.'

'Call me Bob,' I said.

Dead Souls

Camilla Cromwell had been dead for a week before her mind reappeared inside her house. She was a fog of dust and light swirling in the air, awake but not alive, only a presence in her home. She observed her environment, her gaze floating over the contents of the bedroom where she'd died. There was nothing human about her, no signs of arms or legs, of fingers or feet, and when she stared into the mirror, there was no reflection.

I'm a ball of energy.

But she was more of a cloud at first, one that drifted through her empty house. Camilla floated through the bedrooms, observing how different they looked from a higher perspective. Before her death, heights had terrified her, but now she found it peaceful, hovering above everything in this new form.

She stared at the bed where she'd slept alone for over thirty years and peered at the beloved book collection never shared with anyone. Then she went into the spare room, unable to remember why she'd filled it with clothes she'd never worn and jewellery she didn't like.

Then she drifted downstairs, moving through the kitchen hardly used apart from the microwave where Camilla had cooked her frozen meals for one. She thought she could still smell the Bolognese from the day before she died but knew it must have been only a memory. The same with the wine she could taste at the back of her throat.

At least I won't have to worry about drinking too much now.

And this is the most exercise I've had for ages.

Camilla moved out of the kitchen, down the corridor with the Klimt prints on the walls, and into the living room. It was untouched since she'd slid off the sofa, clutching at her chest. She glided down to the floor, convinced she could see an indentation of herself in the carpet.

Perhaps it wasn't a heart attack, and I was killed. But wouldn't the police have outlined my body in the rug?

Camilla shook the idea from the head she no longer had, realising it was because she'd watched far too many crime shows on the TV during her self-enforced imprisonment in the house.

How could anyone have murdered me? Apart from having no enemies – you have to meet people for them to hate you – how would a killer have done it? The food? That was always ordered online and delivered here. Perhaps someone from Tesco held a grudge against me after I sent that email complaining about their last Christmas advert.

Camilla laughed, but she didn't know how she did it, considering she had no throat or mouth. Then she returned her thoughts to all the emails she'd sent over the years. A computer and the internet were godsends to her once her condition became unbearable. She peered at the laptop on the table and drifted towards it. Camilla gazed into the screen, hoping for a reflection of what she was now, but it was empty.

I'm nothing in death. Just like I was in life.

She moved from the computer and settled into the living room window. There was no reflection there either, but somehow she could sense the glass against her. Camilla looked into the garden, staring at the place she hadn't set foot in for thirty years. She'd wanted to go outside so many times: desperate to feel the sun on her face, to hear the birds in the sky, and smell the flowers.

There had been several occasions when Camilla had opened the door, had one foot over the edge, but couldn't move any further. The last few times she'd tried a decade ago, the anxiety had rushed through her like an express train. It had come upon her so suddenly that she'd turned around and thrown up all over the kitchen.

Even now, in this form, I can still smell the regurgitated carrots and cabbage in the room.

Her condition had stopped Camilla from leaving the house, but now her compulsions had disappeared with her body. All those impulses had gone; there was no need to count to two hundred every time she was anxious, no desire to scrub the floor with bleach until her fingers bled, and no urge to stand in the shower for hours until the water scolded her flesh clean.

Perhaps being dead wasn't such a bad thing after all.

That impossible laugh returned.

I had to die to live again.

Camilla's fear of the world had crept up on her, slowly at first. She'd felt the initial tremors of its terrible reach when she was a teenager: the panic attacks when meeting strangers were the first sign. Prescription drugs had helped her get through college and university, but they did their own damage to her mind and body, so much so, she had to reject them eventually.

When the anxiety had increased to the point Camilla froze at the prospect of leaving her home, she knew her only option was to live the rest of her life inside. Working from home and the internet saved her from poverty and insanity, but it was a narrow escape.

Yet every day in the house only amplified the distance between her and the world outside. It was a distance that ate away at Camilla inch by inch. She'd quelled her anxiety, only to replace it with frustration and loneliness.

Now, she could leave and travel to all those places she'd only visited online. She wasn't sure how it worked, but she could move her cloud form; she guessed it was her soul focussing on one direction. Camilla tried it, pressed against the window, thinking she'd drift through it, but it didn't work.

Perhaps I'm not strong enough like this.

Maybe she needed to find a gap or an exit.

She floated through the house with some urgency, hovering through each room in search of a way out. Upstairs and downstairs, she went backwards and forwards, checking every nook and cranny more than once and coming up with nothing. Frustration simmered through her cloudy form, her mind thinking about fingers forming into fists. Growing irritation made her dusty presence vibrate in the air.

And then something remarkable happened.

A group of particles separated from the main cloud and stretched out before her. Camilla watched them swirl around until they became a recognisable outline.

No, it couldn't be, could it?

But it was; an arm forming, then fingers. As she

continued to gaze at it, more of the dust took a solid shape until it developed into a torso and then another arm. The legs and feet followed, and then, even though she couldn't see it, Camilla assumed her head and face completed the body. She moved her hand over her arm and felt nothing; she brought it to her cheeks with the same results. She was a physical presence, yet there was still no reflection.

She knew from the digital clock in her bedroom it had been eight days since her death, a heart attack aged sixty-five, but it appeared nobody had been to the house since they'd carted her away. After that, her solicitor would have disposed of her estate, and it would only be a matter of time before the building was up for sale. Then someone would come and open the door or a window, and she could escape into the world once more.

Yes, death wouldn't be so bad after all.

All Camilla had to do while she waited was find something to stop her from getting bored. She discovered the very thing the next day while realising there was a way in and out of the house somewhere.

The cooing of the pigeon woke her – who knew that dead souls slept – and she floated upstairs to locate the bird. It was on her bed. She scanned the room, searching for how it got it, but finding nothing.

It must be here. Perhaps I could shake the pigeon, and it would fly to the exit.

She drifted above the bird. Camilla reached down as if to grab it, but her fingers passed through its flesh. It was warm and wet inside the animal, the first thing she'd touched, she'd felt, since her death.

The pigeon trembled and then flapped its wings. She held it in her formless fingers as it squirmed in her grasp. It screeched loud enough to disturb the dust in the rafters. It fell through Camilla like confetti at a wedding. Her fear of dirt returned and made her cloudy shoulders shiver.

Camilla watched the dust drift through her and onto the floor, gathering like snow on Christmas Day.

How did I let this room get that dirty?

The bird continued to struggle in her impossible grasp, pushing against her nails and drawing blood. She looked at the blood sink into the carpet, amazed her ghostly form could do that to the pigeon.

I can touch some things.

Everything changed for her with that. The red-spotted stain on the rug reminded her of a Jackson Pollock painting. And she could smell it, that delicious aroma of burnt copper invading the nose she had no more.

The bird twisted its head to glare at her. The fear in its trembling eyes reminded Camilla of all the times she'd been terrified by what was outside her front door.

She was about to pull her fingers out of the bird when she gripped something different. It wasn't blood or muscle or bone, but something else, like holding a small ball of lightning. It warmed her palm and felt wonderful.

Camilla removed her hand, and the pigeon stopped its thrashing, falling onto the bed, dead. She stared at her skin, relaxing her fingers to see the pulsing electric ball of light.

It was the pigeon's soul; it had to be.

As that tickled her mind, the soul flew from her and out of the room. She didn't give it another thought, focussing on the dead pigeon.

Perhaps I could crawl inside it and fly away.

Camilla pushed her head towards the bird, placing her face on its chest and trying to force her way in. Instead, she strained against its flesh, forcing her cheeks along its cold bones. Death trickled across her lips, into her nose and eyes.

It didn't work; she was too big for such a small frame. She sat staring at the corpse for an age, expecting to be disappointed but feeling upbeat. She placed her ghostly fingers over the feathers as a curious idea took shape.

* * *

A week later, the *For Sale* sign went up. She didn't know how long it would take to sell, but she wasn't worried; she had plans to make and experiments to complete. Camilla never discovered how the animals entered the house, but it wasn't long before they wandered into her grasp: more birds, rats, mice, voles, even a few feral cats. It was the same every time she dug her fingers into their flesh; they thrashed around as she found their souls and dragged the pulsing light from them.

Sometimes the soul would linger in her palm for up to a minute, leaving a warm impression on her skin. But most times, it vanished within a second of the creature dying. Camilla wouldn't have a pet or any animal in the house when she was alive, but now she couldn't get enough of them. When she got bored, she tried that same thing on various insects but discovered nothing inside them, only the sensation of something alien crawling over the skin she didn't have anymore.

Unfortunately, the insides of animals, even their ticklish souls, could only entertain her for so long. When not killing animals, she spent most of her time gazing out of the windows. The garden at the back kept her interest going only when she saw an animal there, hoping it would get into the building.

Looking out of the front of the building was more interesting. She watched the neighbours when they were outside, finding herself obsessed with how much time the postman spent inside the house across the street.

Should I go over and tell the husband what his wife has been up to if I get out?

Gossip had held no interest for her when she was alive, but now, in this ghostly form, she desired to leave and interfere with as many lives as possible.

But all she could do was wait.

* * *

It was six months before the property was sold. She'd nearly given up, with her mind on the edge of collapse. She didn't need to talk to people. The last thirty years had proved that to her, but she needed to occupy her brain. Camilla wanted to read, watch, listen, and touch: how much she needed to feel something again that wasn't a dying animal.

Yet, even if she could have grabbed a book or turned on the TV or a computer, all of her possessions were removed two weeks after her demise. She'd followed the removal men around the house, fascinated at how close she could get to them without that familiar feeling of anxiety.

I'm dead. What have I got to be afraid of now?

When they left the front door open, she flew towards it, with glorious expectation filling her. That soon disappeared when her ghostly head smacked against something invisible. That's when she knew she'd never leave the house in that form. Camilla needed a living thing to occupy if she was ever to escape.

And all the animals she'd killed were no good for that.

Then the new owner moved in with his computers and video games, his online gambling, and his job trading stocks and shares over the internet. And when he wasn't doing that, he was outside at, she supposed, his parties and pubs and discos, going by the photos she saw him transferring from his phone to the computer.

He brought no one back to the house, and that disappointed her. His head was unusual, looking like a damaged eraser on the end of a pencil, but she assumed some people found him attractive and amusing. But, if the pictures were genuine, he was spending most of his spare time living as a hedonist.

That was the life she could have if the experiments with the animals worked on him, in his larger form. She wanted to do it immediately, the first day he moved in, but nerves got the better of her, and she skulked away.

Or maybe it was guilt about what she was going to do.

So she worked on that guilt and thought about the years trapped inside those four walls. And of all the years to come.

I might be stuck here for eternity.

That thought was all it took for Camilla to decide it wasn't only animals she'd kill.

I'll do it when he goes to work.

It took her three days to get the plan right in her head, deciding when would be the best time to force her presence inside his body. She'd stopped watching him shower, convincing herself the other times were for research.

If I'm going to use his flesh and bones, I need to know what he looks like undressed.

He strode downstairs, and she let him eat his breakfast first. It was food far too unhealthy for her – fried eggs, bacon, and sausage – but she wanted him to have all of his strength when she stepped inside him. She wasn't worried he'd be able to shake her out of his skin and bones. All she had to do was grab hold of his soul, and he'd be as weak as a kitten.

And I've killed a few of those recently.

Camilla watched him throw the dirty dishes in the sink.

I'll have to clean them later.

Then he went to the door and opened it. She was on him in a flash, pressed against the back of his suit as he lingered in the doorway. The sun was above his head, with birds singing and marshmallow clouds drifting through the sky. She thought of being young again, of experiencing all the pleasures of life.

Of all the things I've missed.

As he put one foot outside, Camilla's mind flooded with memories of before she was ill, when she could leave the house and be with other people.

It was so long ago: the conversations, going to parties, pubs and the cinema. And the gigs I used to go to, dancing and drinking the nights away.

Now she'd have all that again and more.

Camilla didn't know what it would feel like to be inside a male body, but the prospect excited her.

She flexed her ghostly fingers, running them across his back like a pianist ready to perform. Then she pushed them through his clothes, moving past his skin and into the muscle and bone.

Camilla ducked her head through his ribs, smelling the blood flowing through him. His heartbeat increased, vibrating through her and into Camilla's thoughts. It filled her skull, even though she had no skull, like hot water filling a bath. It was terrifying and magnificent at the same time.

That was until she snapped back inside the house like a rubber band, her ghostly howl so loud the tremors ruffled the papers he'd placed on the desk.

She lay on the carpet, watching him leave and close the outside world on her.

Then Camilla peered at the door and realised she could still cry.

* * *

She sat on the floor all day until he returned, legs hunched into her ribs until her chin rested on her knees that weren't there. There was only one way out of this hell, and she knew what it was.

Camilla delayed it for two weeks until he stepped out of the shower one morning. She thrust her hands deep into his chest, finding his heart. It wriggled between her fingers, his thick blood swimming over her translucent skin, as he fell into the wall and screamed. He put up more of a fight than the animals, tearing at his ribs to get her out of him. His nails dug into his skin, ripping at flesh and drawing blood. He continued to wail and claw as she searched for his soul. All the times she'd done this with the animals, she'd found their essence close to their hearts. It was no different with him, discovering the ball of energy hiding inside one of those four chambers.

Camilla grasped the light in her fingers and ripped it from him.

He crashed to the floor, his head cracking against the wall as he slumped onto the tiles. She stood over him, triumphant and grinning. His soul throbbed in her hand until she released her fingers, and it drifted into the air. She watched it float towards the ceiling before plunging her form into him, pushing apart his ribs, cells, and settling into his chest, unfurling herself deep in his heart. She stretched out her arms and legs as if she was trying on a new suit.

This feels wonderful.

She lay there inside him, taking in the warmth of his body, feeling the blood pumping through his veins. Her soul had replaced his like changing the battery in a mobile phone. Camilla stared at the ceiling and then pushed herself up.

But she didn't move.

Nothing moved, no matter how hard she tried. And she tried minute after minute, hour after hour.

* * *

The police broke into the house forty-eight hours later. The paramedics removed him, took the body away, and straight to the nearest hospital. She peered out of unmoving eyes, and several medical staff poked and prodded him. Their lips moved, but she couldn't hear what they said.

Something has happened to my ears.

She watched one nurse take a needle and stick it into her arm. Then the darkness came for Camilla.

Her hearing returned in the night when a terrible scream woke her.

But she still couldn't move or speak.

The next morning, she overheard the medics talking about the cerebral aneurysm he'd had in the brain.

'How long will he be in a coma?' One doctor said to the other.

'He'll probably never come out of it,' was the reply.

When Camilla screamed, she could have sworn one of those doctors heard her.

But they just walked away.

And she gazed at the ceiling and saw all the dust there.

Road To Nowhere

Eddie Parker grinned as he slit another throat. He dragged the blade across the man's flesh, slicing into the badly drawn skull tattoo. The blood gushed everywhere, staining the walls, the furniture, the TV, and covering the books scattered over the carpet. He pushed out his cheeks, taking a deep breath and tasting weak beer and stale pizza at the back of his mouth. His crimson hand ached as much as the throb sprinting down his spine.

Anticipation gripped his soul now he was so close to his goal. He let go, and the man slumped to the floor, another corpse in Eddie's long journey. He reached down, searching through a dead man's clothes for the thing he'd killed so many for.

But it wasn't there.

'Fuck!'

Eddie moved from the body and headed for the door, but couldn't progress without the key. He placed a hand on the exit, knowing there was only one more chance before everything crumbled around him.

Again.

'Fucking stuck in this place forever.'

He blinked twice, trying to remove the haze covering his eyes and the fog sinking into his brain. He stayed frozen to the spot, uncertainty replacing the blood in his veins. Only the banging on the door sparked him into action.

'Let me in, Eddie.'

He dropped the game controller, moving his legs for the first time in hours, and peered at his avatar on the screen. There were matching confused looks on both faces: one of flesh, the other of digital pixels.

The woman crashed her fist against the door again. 'I swear to God, Eddie.'

His whole body ached as he let her in before she disturbed the neighbours.

Annie Bishop stumbled into the flat, glancing around the room before heading straight for his booze. She poured herself a large whisky while he scrutinised her. She had eyes like burnt cigarettes, a fire blazing inside her that worried him. He knew why she was there.

She downed half of the alcohol. 'You're a lying piece of shit, Eddie.'

He flexed his hand to lessen the pain caused by holding the game controller for so long.

'You'd have done the same, Annie, if I hadn't got there first.'

She slammed the glass onto the desk. 'You stole my code, claimed it as yours, and told everyone I'm only a script kiddie.' She glared at him. 'Are you that desperate for the money?'

He shook his head and laughed. 'It's not about the cash, Annie. It's never been about the financial rewards.'

She poured herself another drink. 'Then what is it? Is it to humiliate me because I won't fuck you anymore?'

Eddie licked at the sides of his mouth, finding a stray piece of yesterday's cheese pizza. He'd always imagined she'd be more attractive when angry, with her long dark hair flowing behind her like a dragon ready to devour everything in its path. But now, as he stared at the hate seeping from Annie, he wondered what he'd seen in her.

His legs throbbed as he watched her. 'Sex? That's so overrated. Any moron can get laid.' Eddie flexed his fingers as he stepped towards her. 'All I've ever wanted is recognition and respect, and now I have it.'

She shook her head. 'Respect? You stole my fucking work. How does that get you respect?'

He looked at her from top to bottom. 'Where's your phone? You're not recording this, are you?'

Annie reached into her pocket and removed a packet of cigarettes. She lit one and blew the smoke into his face.

'I should have known what you'd do since you're such a slimy git.'

He touched his chest and coughed. 'You know I don't like you smoking in here.'

She blasted more smoke his way. 'Why should I care what you think?' Her hand trembled as she stubbed the cigarette on his sofa. 'I've got all the original code stored on a hard drive, dated well before you claimed it as yours. I'll post it online unless you tell the world the truth.'

'Who else knows this?'

She flicked the stub onto the floor. 'Nobody, of course.' Annie glanced at the TV screen and smiled. 'And you still can't get beyond level nine. That's because of me.'

Eddie was close enough to smell the jasmine in her hair. 'Where's the key in that room? It's not on the last guardian, and I've searched everywhere else.' A cruel suspicion crawled through his mind. 'Did you add the key to the final level?'

Her grin irritated him. 'I thought *you* completed all that code, Eddie? I'm only a script kiddie, remember?'

Then he realised. 'This version isn't finished, is it?'

Annie shrugged. 'I think deep down I knew you'd screw me over; that's why I held something back.'

'But it's on this hard drive you mentioned?'

She didn't answer. 'You know why I left home and came to the city?'

Eddie nodded. 'You wanted a better life.'

'It was more than that,' she said. 'There was an illness in the village, but it wasn't one of chemistry or biology unless you believed bigotry was inherent inside human DNA. It was accompanied by a secondary disease, that of silence. These twin ailments didn't affect everyone, but they affected enough. Eventually, I viewed its inhabitants as no more than the living dead, walking emotional corpses to avoid. My biggest fear was being caught there forever. That's why I was so happy when I found someone who'd gone through the same thing. Or at least they claimed they did.'

'It wasn't a lie, Annie. If I hadn't left home, I would have been stuck in a rut, doing the same as my father and his father before him, sitting in an office pushing papers around until I died. That's what happened to them. So I took off and followed my dreams of creating new realities, of entertaining the masses.'

Her lips curled up as she spoke. 'But you couldn't do that without my help.'

'Is the final code on the hard drive, Annie?'

The glint in her eyes told him he was right. And she wouldn't have the drive with her; it would be in that flat they'd shared before she kicked him out. That realisation decided his next move.

Eddie grabbed the porcelain figure of Lara Croft from the bookshelf and hit Annie on the side of her head. It split against her skull, sending Annie into the wall and floor. He towered over her, watching the blood consume her eyes as her lips trembled. He didn't give her a chance to say anything, bending to strike again. By the time he'd finished, his fingers were hidden in red, and nothing remained of her face. He left her there and poured himself a drink. Then he slumped onto the sofa, staring at the screen and his frozen avatar, searching for the one thing that would propel him to the next level. He recognised, not for the first time, that it was a metaphor for his life.

He was ten years old when he realised something was different about him compared to the other kids. His father's disdain for Eddie and his mother's hate bothered him until he understood they were as worthless as everybody else. His epiphany arrived that night in the woods when he cracked open Billy Madison's skull and the pleasure he got from watching his friend wriggle on the ground like a chopped-up worm. The adults believed a stranger must have attacked Billy, so Eddie went about his life with nobody the wiser. Little Billy never recovered - still in a coma to this day - so Eddie's murderous indiscretions were kept well-hidden as they had been ever since, even with the others he'd killed.

And that was why he didn't panic when he gazed at Annie's corpse on his carpet. It would be an easy problem to solve. First, he'd dispose of her body in the woods where he'd put the others – the same place he'd attacked Billy so long ago. Then go to the flat they used to share and find the hard drive she mentioned. Finally, with the completed code, he'd get the key and finish the game before presenting it to the investors.

He gazed at the blood pooling around her head, smiling because she'd landed right in the middle of the carpet, so it would be easy to wrap her in it. All he needed to do was wait until his neighbour left for work and then move her to the garage and into the car with nobody seeing him.

Eddie finished his drink before searching Annie's clothes, removing her mobile and keys. He'd dump the phone in the river once he'd buried her and retrieved the hard drive. Then he had a shower and went for a nap, glancing at his frozen avatar on the screen as he headed to the bedroom.

Three hours later, he whistled along to Kate Bush on the radio as he drove along the country road to the woods. He rubbed at the broken nail he'd acquired while heaving the carpeted body into the boot. It irritated his finger, but at least he'd got Annie out of the house and into the vehicle unseen.

Eddie tapped his fingers on the wheel to the music while the boot's contents rumbled behind him. The drive would only take an hour, getting deeper into the country-side before reaching the woods. Twenty years ago, his family had lived in the village near the trees, and he could walk there from his house in ten minutes. Now, it was a familiar trip along narrow country tracks and hidden lanes.

The landscape lay before him like an old friend, curving and changing like the lines and ridges of his hands. The dip and sway of the land, the patterns and shapes of the trees and bushes guided Eddie on his journey. The roads were a fine black ink cutting through nature's green. He wound down the window, taking in the night air, listening to the wind sweep across the car. Its calmness added to his own, the empty lanes reminding him of the isolation of his childhood. He'd hated the loneliness and lack of love then, but he knew now it had strengthened him for the transition into adulthood.

The tyres bounced over the bumps in the road, forcing the body to shuffle around in the boot. The noise annoyed him, so he increased the volume on the radio, listening to Jagger dancing on dead butterflies as he sang about not getting what he wanted.

Eddie pictured himself eating a Mars Bar with Marianne Faithfull when a woman stepped in front of the car. He swerved to avoid her, the tyres screeching across the surface, twisting his back in agony as he slammed on the brakes. The wheels stopped in a ditch as he jerked into the steering wheel. He undid the seatbelt, opened the door, and stumbled out. Buzzing tiny flies brushed his face as he threw up in the bushes. Yesterday's pizza rushed up his guts and all over the green surrounding him. He leant forward, one hand pushed into the bark of the nearest tree. It cut into his skin and drew blood as he vomited again.

He finished and lifted his head, wiping his arm across his mouth. Then he turned, searching for the woman who'd forced him off the road. However, apart from the car, the only illumination around him came from the moon and the stars. He lingered in the gloom, seeing nobody and wondering if he must have hit her and knocked her into a ditch.

Eddie grabbed his phone to turn on the torch, but the battery had died.

'Fuck!'

His legs and arms felt like he'd been lifting weights all

day. He took a cursory look into the ditch, but since the woman wasn't there, he returned to the car. Jagger was still singing as Eddie closed the door and drove away.

The drive comforted him, glad to be back on a familiar route.

But he'd only gone two hundred yards when he saw the woman again, standing at the side of the road. He slowed this time, looking closely at her: she wore a long white dress that shimmered in the darkness, with straight black hair resting on her heart. Eddie stopped as he got to her, pain shooting through his ribs when he saw her face.

Annie!

He thrust a hand to his throat, trying to get the breath that had abandoned him

It couldn't be her.

Her eyes gazed into his, pushing through his retinas and diving into the four chambers of his trembling heart.

Then she vanished.

He got out of the car, scanning the surroundings to ensure he wasn't hallucinating. Eddie sucked in the aromas of the flowers and the bushes, hearing the trickle of the running water from the nearby stream. Tall strands of wheat swayed in the meadow beyond the bank, undulating like waves crashing into sand, revealing a withered scarecrow staring at him. An obsidian crow sat on its head, its shape only discernible because of the flickering moon behind it.

He turned from its gaze to where the woman had stood. Eddie scrutinised the ground, searching for signs of life, footprints, or anything she might have dropped, but there was nothing. He waited for the tremble in his legs to subside before moving to the Errington Woods sign. The wood pricked his fingers as he ran them across it, letting the blood drip to guarantee all of this was real and not a figment of his imagination.

Eddie lifted his hand to his mouth, tasting the bitterness of his flesh. Then he took a deep breath, glanced at the unmoving moon, and went to the rear of the car. He drank cold air like a vampire, opening the boot and expecting it to be empty. It wasn't. He removed the knife from his pocket and cut the bindings at the top of the carpet. He pulled them back and peered into Annie's dead eyes. Then he inched more of the rug away, satisfied to see she wore a jacket and trousers. There was no long white dress.

A figment of his imagination, that's what it must have been.

He'd never had a reaction like this after previous murders, but he had been staring at the TV screen for hours on end this time, trying to get to the last level of that stupid game.

The game. He'd lied to her about it. It wasn't all about respect; he wanted all the money. He needed it to pay off his gambling debts.

Eddie gazed into her dead eyes again, knowing what the game's final name would be.

Eddie's Quest.

Yes, that would be perfect.

He smiled and closed the boot. The crow continued to stare at him from the scarecrow's head, but he didn't care. Whatever he'd seen had been a momentary aberration caused by lack of sleep.

But it would soon be over, and he'd get plenty of rest then.

Eddie drove away, feeling good about himself again. Until he realised the Stones were still singing the same tune.

He changed the station several times but kept getting that same song. Then he glanced out of the window, seeing the Errington Woods sign. The one he'd cut his fingers on.

Eddie stopped the car and switched off the radio. His heart thumped against his ribs, threatening to burst out of him. He got out and looked across the road, peering at the bird and the scarecrow gazing back at him. The moon hadn't moved. He examined his hand, finding his blood still there.

Then he sensed the presence behind him.

Every hair on Eddie's arms and neck sprang to attention. The wind chilled his face as the sweat dripped from his forehead. He didn't want to move, his legs ignoring his brain, but he knew it was better to know what was there than not.

The car radio blared as he turned, his head down and peering at the ground. He glimpsed the bottom of the white dress first, his gaze rising to see the dark hair resting on her chest. Invisible fingers clutched at his heart when he saw her face, the chill speeding through his bones at Annie's smile.

How was this possible?

Her mouth opened, and a swarm of flies came out. He lifted his arm for protection, and the insects buzzed around his head before flying into the distance.

'You should have got the key before you killed me, Eddie.'

His whole body shook as he reached for her, the blood still clinging to his fingers. Eddie's breath froze in the air as he inched forward, his hand close to her cheek.

Then she vanished.

Eddie stood there, his arm lingering in the empty space.

He closed his eyes, took three deep breaths, and opened them again.

It was a dream, that's all. Perhaps he should rest in the car before continuing.

But what if somebody came along? The police, maybe. The road was out of the way and got little traffic, especially at night, but it would be just his luck if the coppers arrived. No, he had to keep going. The woods weren't far away. The sign told him that.

That sign. He'd driven past the same one twice. That wasn't possible. Was there more than one on this stretch of the road? He couldn't remember, but there had to be.

He went to the car, refusing to stare at the scarecrow. Jagger warbled out of the radio, so Eddie turned the volume to a whisper. He didn't fasten his seatbelt and drove off. He'd travelled a hundred yards when he saw the sign again. He stopped and got out, moving straight to the rear. The car creaked as he opened the boot, peering at Annie's face where he'd removed the carpet.

'How are you doing this, Annie?'

No answer came.

He closed the boot and stared at the spot where he'd seen her in the white dress. She wasn't there. The radio increased in volume, and Jagger's voice echoed into the night.

Eddie went to the Errington Woods sign and touched the dried blood on it. His dried blood. Then he looked at the crow and the scarecrow peering at him from underneath the frozen moon.

That's when Eddie Parker knew he'd be stuck at that level forever.

Cry Wolf

Tommy Wolf reread the headline.

'Sex and drugs and rock and roll: local politician's scandalous secret.'

It was old news, two decades ago, but he knew people would click the text to read the rest of it, a not-too-uncommon tale of a teenage musician who had a dalliance with a seaside shop assistant. Unfortunately, the girl would die in a tragic accident a few years later, while the aspiring Elvis became the local Member of Parliament. There was nothing to the story apart from the fact that the right honourable gentleman was now the leading spokesperson for the Party, proclaiming the return to Family Values.

'Whatever they are?' Tommy said to the energetic-looking pigeon peering at him through the window. None of it mattered; he only cared about the thousands who would click through and generate the advertising revenue that paid for his comfortable lifestyle.

'Thank goodness for tabloid trash and fake news.' He slammed his hand against the glass, and the bird tumbled backwards towards the cracked pavement below. 'And all those who sail through its murky pages.' His gaze returned to the computer, with the pointer hovering over the Publish button, before he started his usual five-second ritual.

'Think of the lives you'll ruin,' he said, perfectly impersonating the editor he'd sacked two years ago. He grinned and hit the button, leaning into his chair and lighting an imaginary cigar, hand clutching the mouse as he scanned the contents on the large digital screen.

While waiting for the first results to return, he browsed through the viewed pages on his *Wolf Crier* website. Initially, he'd thought the name was too corny when the web designer suggested it, but he realised how appropriate it was once he considered it.

'I am a kind of town crier,' he told his wife before she left him for the sacked editor. 'And newspapers often have the word crier in the title,' he told a barman who ignored him while pouring out Tommy's sixth whisky on a busy afternoon.

'And my name is Wolf,' the cracked reflection in the mirror mumbled at him. So the title stuck, and his site regularly hit the top ten internet searches for the latest news. While that was good for business, it generated an ongoing dilemma – constantly having to create clickable stories. In a journalistic career reaching back thirty years, Tommy had never been averse to stretching the truth until it resembled something from an alternate universe. Most of his staff had a problem with it, so he sacked them on the spot, replacing them with bloggers who'd do anything to be a proper journalist. He laughed at the thought of it.

'What about people who complain?' a new staffer asked him.

'Simple,' he replied. 'We'll have a page where we print apologies and retractions, but with a link so small and buried so deep in the site nobody will find it.' He was pleased with his ingenuity and deviousness.

'If you keep publishing copy like this, nobody will believe you.' Tommy found the kid annoying, but at least he did his job.

'Nobody cares anymore,' Tommy said.

He stared again at the screen as the hits increased – six hundred clicks in the first few minutes. Inside his head, the sounds of a cash register made him happy. As the numbers grew, he wondered if his latest gossamer gossip would make it into the most-viewed stories on the site. Political posts comprised fifty per cent of the list; the others were a mixture of crime and celebrity blather. He scanned them from top to bottom and counted the profits in his mind before reading the best five.

The Pope's Baby. The comments section was hardly gracious. He'd never expected so many religious people to swear at him in such ingenious ways.

Morgue Worker Arrested After Giving Birth to a Dead Man's Baby. The creeps and perverts came out in hordes for that piece. The couple had been married, but he buried that nugget in the small print on the retraction's page.

Woman Arrested For Defecating On Boss' Desk After Winning The Lottery. The poor woman had been sick when she'd heard about winning ten million, but the headline made a much better story.

Clown Rob's Bank and Escapes in Tiny Car. That one made the rounds when there was a spate of real stories in the news about people in creepy clown masks wandering the streets.

Magician Ate my Hamster. It was the tale of an annoyed magician's assistant, but no animals were actually harmed.

His gaze returned to the part of the screen with the latest analytical data, happy with the knowledge there'd been a thousand clicks and over five hundred shares in just over ten minutes. Then, confident it would only get better in the next few hours, he turned to the section on the computer where he stored his upcoming stories for the next one because if he rested on his laurels, he'd be left behind or usurped by the other sites.

'Bingo!' he said when he found the folder about the celeb with an alleged gambling addiction. The light in his eyes was fiercer than the sun as he clicked through the minimal gossip an apprentice had acquired. However, Tommy was glad of that – the more gaps there were, the more creative he could be.

He let go of the mouse, pressed his hands together and pondered the headline. Everything else would easily follow as long as the clickbait was enticing enough. He concentrated so hard on the task he didn't notice there was somebody with him. The sudden smell of rotten eggs made Tommy turn from the computer to see the stranger sitting behind him.

'We're not hiring, so get out.' It was Tommy's automatic reflex when new people turned up in the office. Not that the woman opposite him looked desperate enough to work for the *Wolf Crier*. She was the perfect specimen with arctic blue eyes and long blonde hair. He ignored her and returned to his screen, before remembering he'd locked the door. 'How did you get in?' He swivelled the chair to face the intruder.

'I need you for a job, Tommy. Can I call you Tommy? It will last many years; to start immediately.'

Tommy's nostrils flexed as he snorted like a pneumatic pig. 'I don't work for the opposition.'

'Well,' the stranger said. 'I represent a unique organisation; you could say we are the originators of the information you disseminate.' Tommy was about to laugh when he noticed the intruder's eyes had changed from cold blue to fiery red. He blinked, thinking he'd imagined it, but when his vision cleared, he still saw those burning eyes gazing back at him.

'Who are you?'

'My organisation has a long history, but we've been quiet for a while, and I require someone with your specific skills to promote the work we're about to undertake. It's a big job, highly pressurised, but I believe you'll be able to handle it.'

'I'm not interested,' Tommy said, trying to be assertive but hearing his voice sounding like a small child's.

'I'm not here to bargain with you; your contract started fifteen minutes ago. When you hit that Publish button, your agreement was transferred to my organisation.'

'What agreement?' Tommy said, as the hits on his latest news story pushed past ten thousand. The stranger shifted in her lilac-coloured trousers, juniper-hued shirt, dapper waistcoat and crimson jacket as she glanced around the office.

'Oh, you know it's in some old book somewhere; you'll have read it as a kid.'

Tommy slumped into his chair, the realisation of what was happening sinking in. 'I didn't sign any contract; this isn't fair.' His voice came in short bursts, his heart pumping faster than it should have been.

'I'll give you a chance, Tommy. Post a new story on your website and, in the first sixty seconds, if one of your readers believes it to be true, I'll search for a different Head of Communications at my organisation.'

Tommy's pulse slowed, his eager brain seeing an escape from his terrible, imminent fate. He turned to the computer and pulled up a new page, fingers hovering over the keyboard.

'Okay,' he said, 'what's the headline?' His smile returned, knowing that, however ludicrous the tale, at least one of his avid followers would believe the truth of it.

The stranger left her chair and stood at Tommy's shoulder, hot breath streaming over his skin.

'*Website owner gets a job in Hades.*'

Tommy's fingers skimmed over the keys without his doing and typed those words. Two more paragraphs followed, even though he had no control over what he did.

Then he clicked the Publish button.

As the sixty seconds counted down Tommy saw the stranger's face fluctuate between woman, cherub, eagle, and lion. He tried not to cry and waited for that one user to believe what he'd written.

It was an eternal wait.

Monsters of Mars

Fifty years after the colonisation of Mars, war erupted on the red planet.

Emma Hart touched the bruises under her eyes. Then she stared at the room where her captors had dragged her for the interrogation. Because of the conditions on Mars, human survival required living in artificial habitats with complex life-support systems. The first of these had been built on the surface, but twenty years after the first humans had set foot on the planet, most were underground. This provided easier access to the water beneath the earth while protecting the population from the harshness above.

Emma had been born in such a place, and now she expected to die in one.

The walls were white stone, with random spots of dark on them, which Emma guessed might have been blood. There was a lingering smell of death in the air. She shook her head at the realisation the enemy, who were winning the war, were less hygienic than her people.

My people. Their people. But we're all humans.

The lights flickered in the room, and she wondered how

successful the attack on the electricity supply had been. Conflict was complicated on the red planet, for one wrong move could destroy something essential to everyone surviving on Mars, not just the enemy. That was why both sides had to pick their targets carefully.

And that's how they'd caught her.

She glanced at the table with three people sitting at it. In front of it was an empty seat, waiting for her. Next to that was a large covered object.

The armed guard pushed her towards the chair. She wiped the blood from her swollen lip as she stumbled into it, peering at her captors and trying not to think about her husband and daughter.

'Be careful with our honoured guest, Jack.'

Emma recognised the speaker as Erasmus, the enemy leader. Jack went to restrain her hands, but Erasmus shook his head.

'I don't think there's any need for that. Is there, Dr Hart?'

Emma rubbed at the pain in her wrist. 'Is that because you'll be letting me go soon?'

Erasmus laughed. 'Of course, Emma.' He grinned at her. 'Can I call you Emma?'

She didn't reply as he turned to the two sitting with him: a woman with dead eyes, short white hair, and a bald man who couldn't stop picking at his teeth.

'I'm sorry about what happened to your face, Dr Hart,' the woman said. Emma didn't think she was sorry at all.

Erasmus continued to smile. 'I'm sure Emma knows everything is fair in love and war.'

Emma returned his grin. 'This isn't love.'

Erasmus nodded. 'Of course it is Emma. This is true love.' He pointed to the guard, who pressed a button in his hand. The wall on the side slid up to reveal a glass partition looking into another room. Emma peered into it, unable to see what was there until a body jerked up, and she saw a man sitting next to a table. He was restrained, with wires connected to his head, arms, and legs.

'Alan,' she whispered.

Erasmus stood and removed the cover near Emma, revealing a machine similar to the one in the next room.

'I've never been married, Dr Hart, but is it true that husbands and wives are better suited when they have the same interests?'

She struggled to control her breathing. 'What are these machines?'

The bald man stood. 'My name is Carpenter, Dr Hart, and the Liquidator is my invention.'

Emma's heart thumped against her ribs. 'Liquidator?'

Carpenter winced. 'It's not my choice of name.' He glanced at the white-haired woman. 'That was Gemma's idea, but at least it's appropriate.'

Emma couldn't take her eyes from her husband in the other room. 'What does it do?'

Carpenter rubbed his hands together as if trying to start a fire. 'Do you know how a microwave cooks from the inside out?' She nodded. 'Well, that's what the Liquidator does, simmering the blood and organs until the boiling point turns the subject into a melting mess.'

Erasmus leaned towards her. 'Contrary to what you people think, we here at the Institute are not monsters.' His ocean-blue eyes gazed at her. 'But we will do whatever is necessary to protect ourselves.'

'As shall we,' Emma said.

'So you understand the severity of our situation and

what will happen to you and the man in the other room if you don't answer our questions?'

She glanced at Alan. 'Of course.'

Erasmus settled into his chair. 'Good, good. So you'll tell me which of our people let the two of you into this facility.'

Emma laughed. 'Nobody let us in. We were out for a stroll, enjoying the sunset, when we spotted the door to the underground open. So we thought, why not visit our neighbours to see if they're not as horrible as we were led to believe.'

The dead-eyed woman, Gemma, moved across the table and slapped Emma hard. Emma's cheeks burnt red with pain, but she didn't flinch.

'One more lie from you, and we burn the man in the next room. Do you understand?'

Emma rubbed at her skin and nodded. She glanced at Alan, knowing neither of them would leave alive.

'We killed two of your people to get in here. Then we headed down a corridor towards the generator, but your guards stopped us.'

Erasmus peered at her as if she was some new species he'd just discovered. 'You intended to turn off the life support, was that it?' She didn't reply, content to let him play it out in his mind. 'Your environment suits would have provided you with oxygen to survive. What would you have done then? Returned up top to allow more of your people in here to finish any survivors?'

'It sounded a good enough plan,' Emma said.

'I don't believe you, Dr Hart. Why would the enemy send a scientist on such a mission?' He glanced at Alan through the glass. 'Your husband isn't a fighter; he's a biologist like you.'

She kept her eyes on the man interrogating her. 'We volunteered for this. We knew what we were getting into.'

'I'm not sure you did,' Erasmus said as he nodded to the guards in the other room.

Emma turned as a guard flicked a switch on the machine connected to her husband. She could have looked away but didn't, staring into the face of the only man she'd ever loved.

Even with the walls and the glass between them, she smelt burning flesh as the power increased next door. Alan was still until his body jerked forward and fought against his restraints. Blood dripped from his eyes and mucus from his nose. His cheeks bulged, transforming from white into dark grey instantly. Alan's arms twisted into an unnatural shape as he struggled against what the machine was doing to him. Emma imagined she heard his wrists snap as he bent them against the straps holding him down. Smoke came from his mouth as she finally turned from the horror.

'He's not dead yet,' Erasmus said. 'Even with the machine switched off, his blood and internal organs will boil. The brain may continue for a couple more minutes when his heart stops. Perhaps his last thought might be of you and your pointless sacrifice.'

Emma bit the top of her tongue. 'We could have lived together in peace.'

Erasmus shook his head. 'It's far too late for that, Dr Hart.'

She glared at him. 'Is that why your soldiers slaughtered everyone at our Hellas Planitia outpost?'

'It was a legitimate target. Just like you and your husband sneaking in here to kill us.'

Blood slipped into Emma's mouth. 'My daughter, Victoria, was there. She was six years old.'

Erasmus shrugged. 'There are no innocents in war, Emma.'

She peered at her hand before glancing at her husband. 'I know.'

Then she stared at her captors, wondering who would react first.

It was the woman, Gemma, clutching at her cheek. 'What's..., what's happening?'

She fell from the chair, her legs sprawled on the floor as the others jumped up. Emma glanced through the glass into the room, watching the guards silently collapse.

Then the gunman behind her stumbled into the wall, his face turning purple as he clawed at his cheeks. Carpenter reached out to Erasmus, who moved away from his stricken colleague.

'Is this your doing?' Erasmus said to her.

Emma stood and answered his question. 'You build killing machines, but we built a virus.'

The startled man gazed at his dying colleagues on the floor. 'It's impossible to get a bio-weapon into this facility. Our sensors scanned you and your husband as soon as you entered: both of you are clean.'

She went to the glass and put her hand on it, peering at the body of the man she loved. 'That's the beauty of what we created; it only spreads from human cells once they're dead.' She glanced at the ceiling. 'Your excellent ventilation system did the rest.' Emma smiled at Erasmus. 'You must be stronger than the others, but I guess you'll feel it in your veins now.'

He fell into the table, holding the chair for support. 'You sacrificed yourself for this?'

'The antidote is in my blood, but we knew one or both of us would have to die to end this war.'

Erasmus collapsed as the blood ran from his eyes and mouth. She didn't give him another thought as she stepped over him and went to the door. She stopped there before returning to get the dead guard's gun.

Then she moved into the corridor, ready to see how effective her virus had been.

Books of Brilliant Things

Joanna stopped playing with jigsaws on her tenth birthday when her mother gave her one of the *Texas Chainsaw Massacre*. Not that it scared her, more that Joanna finally realised she was the biggest puzzle in her life.

She sought answers to that enigma but discovered nothing to satisfy her curious and energetic mind. It was only in reading – starting with comics and magazines before moving on to books – that she found solace in a painful existence.

And it was ironic that her introduction to fiction began with real physical pain when her mother dropped a copy of the *Complete Works of William Shakespeare* – leather-bound – on Joanna's foot. She hadn't realised how many obscenities were hiding in her unconscious until then. Still, it set her off on a world of discovery from which she had never looked back.

Joanna became a devoted reader, but it wasn't until she started walking everywhere that she discovered how many stories she could get through in a week. Her day would begin with a raw egg and burnt toast as she perused what unread book she had left in her tiny flat. Then, once she decided what to read, she would set off with a smile, ensuring she avoided the strange neighbour who kept asking her if she wanted to watch a movie with him. In her long-forgotten past she'd craved company, but it had been ages since she'd had it – she didn't count the infrequent visits to her mother in prison – that Joanna wouldn't know what to do if she got it.

Reading while walking had seemed impossible, considering how clumsy she was. Her lumbering, gawky gait was why she had so many bruises – so she told her teachers, and they believed her. Or they didn't care. But she was bruise-free when she arrived at university, where she discovered the Read and Walk club.

Those first few days on campus had been a revelation to her. For one, she was getting away from her family, but more importantly, to realise that other people treasured books as much as she did. Even though the Read and Walk club faced ridicule from most of the other students and several staff members, it gave Joanna the self-belief to do what she loved the most, regardless of what others thought of her. Sure, there may have been some untimely accidents in her initial excursions, like when she walked into that dog or fell into a pothole, but she finally felt alive with a book in her hands and the wind in her hair as she kept on walking.

Striding through the quiet boulevards as she lost herself in words on the page was what she lived for. It was the perfect way to start the day, and she could clear her mind of the nightmares and restless sleep by immersing herself in those pages. Even bad weather wouldn't stop her from reading while walking. A constant downpour would only slow her pace, giving her more time to read. The air would be damp and humid, and the ground wet and slippery, yet still she strode on. The streets and sidewalks were slick and shiny, and puddles formed in low-lying areas. Umbrellas would spring up everywhere around her, people grimacing in raincoats and waterproof boots as water splashed over her current book. But she embraced the whole experience, revelling in how nature became part of her outdoor reading routine.

Sometimes lightning and thunder accompanied the rain, adding to the drama and intensity. Mary Shelley's *Frankenstein* was one of her favourites to read in a downpour. She knew some people listened to music while they read – audiobooks were the devil to her – but she preferred listening to nature as the words formed in her mind. Joanna thought nothing could distract her while strolling through the village – barking dogs, alluring women, and brawling men had all tried and failed – but one day, something did.

That was when she discovered the street library.

Joanna was a woman of little financial means, living in a cheap but cheerful one-bedroomed flat where the heating didn't work in the coldest months, and all the neighbours had missing teeth, so her books came from the public library. But because of government cuts, they stocked fewer items by the month and were only open half the time they used to be.

So when she discovered the street library near the dilapidated train station – down to only six journeys a day – she nearly had a heart attack. She didn't even know what a street library was until the train driver sneaking a crafty fag by the public toilets told her.

'It's a way to share books with strangers,' he said. 'Without having to meet them. The people, not the books.'

That was double good news, since she had been terrified of strangers since childhood. Her mother had warned Joanna every day not to talk to outsiders.

'Or they'll whisk you away and pull your eyes out,' she told Joanna. 'And they'll eat them in front of you, but you won't be able to see because the stranger will spread your eyes on toast with dollops of butter, and drinking wine while you lay on the floor, curled up like a baby and whining.'

So sharing her passion with others without meeting them sounded perfect. The first time she saw the street library, her heart lit up; two wooden boxes filled with books perched on a bench. The train driver was only a few yards away, blowing smoke in the air. Once he told her why the books were there, she slipped her current read – Anna Burns's *Milkman* – into her jacket pocket and inched towards that unexpected treasure.

She reached in and carefully pulled out a book, running her fingers over the spine. It was a mystery novel, Agatha Christie's *The Mystery of the Blue Train*. The cover was frayed at the edges, showing a brown-hatted man carrying an unconscious woman in his arms.

I doubt the publisher would get away with that today.

Still, it was eye-catching. She flicked through the other books, her heart thumping against her chest as if she was on a first date, not that she could remember having her only first date since it was so long ago. There were novels, non-fiction, poetry, and plays waiting for her. She felt like a kid in a candy store, resisting the temptation to take one more book and then another. So instead, she settled for the Christie, the latest Ian Rankin, and a biography of Frida Kahlo. Joanna clutched them in her arms, the pages easing her beating heart, and took them home. And it never rained once.

Joanna visited the street library once a week, returning the previous books and acquiring new ones. Then, after a month, somebody replaced the boxes with a converted kitchen cabinet, a two-door, four-shelf storage space painted blue with yellow edges and "FREE BOOKS" stencilled on one side. It smelt of pine needles. She didn't know who owned the street library, and for the first few months, she didn't care, but the longer she spent utilising it, the more she wondered. In all of her visits, increased to twice weekly, not once had she seen anybody else use it.

Where are all the books coming from? And who takes the ones I leave?

She thought, at one point, about leaving messages inside the front covers, so perhaps instigating a conversation with the other, unknown book lovers. But then the idea worried her.

What if somebody wants more than I can give?

Finally, after two months of browsing and an accumulated read through crime, mystery, thrillers, fantasy, science fiction, paranormal romance and erotica novels, history, biographies, politics, economics, and nature, she met somebody at the street library: another woman. Her first instinct was to assume it was safer than meeting a strange man, but Joanna's upbringing had taught her that women could be just as dangerous as men.

The woman stared at Joanna through watery eyes, a formidable figure with a sturdy frame and wrinkly face. Her long, white hair was pulled back into a tight bun, and she wore a threadbare dress that hung off her bony shoulders. Yet, despite her advanced age, her voice was deep and robust, like the rumble of thunder on a summer's day.

'Have you seen any Sylvia Day novels here?' the woman said.

'Sylvia Day?'

Her eyes narrowed as she peered at Joanna. 'She writes erotic fiction. It's just what I need to warm up my nights. And afternoons.'

'No,' Joanna said. 'Sorry.'

The woman waved her hand at invisible furies. 'No matter, as long as it's not our latest MP trying to get this removed.'

'Remove the street library? Why?'

The woman's laugh erupted from her mouth like volcanic lava. 'As the great Terry Pratchett once said, stories of imagination tend to upset those without one.'

Joanna grinned. 'Indeed, but that seems harsh.' She gazed at the books like Romeo fawning over Juliet. 'There must be more to it than that.'

'Of course, he hates anybody having anything for free. The likes of him believe the only worth in life is wealth and how much you have. Most terrible politicians have a fundamental disingenuousness about their politics; the ideologies they trumpet blatantly serve as masks for craven greed or outright bigotry, existing to be quietly discarded when and if they contradict these real goals. They seek to enrich themselves, their friends and donors, while fuelling a vicious desire to hurt people. This does not make them more or less dangerous; it is simply a thing that is generally true about their ideology.'

Joanna stared at the woman, perplexed.

My mother was right; people are strange. No wonder I generally avoid talking to them.

'Well, I hope he doesn't get his way. I'll be lost without the street library.'

The woman rifled through the latest deposits: hardcover books on archaeology and cooking, a clothbound coffee-table book on spells and witchcraft, some young adult fantasy fiction and Alan Moore's *Jerusalem*.

She grabbed the spells and witchcraft. 'Perhaps we should put a spell on the bastard. What do you think of that?'

Joanna laughed until she saw the woman wasn't joking. She took a deep breath and glanced at the Moore novel.

'I've always believed that literature, fiction, is magic; a way to enchant others: sometimes to win their hearts or even make them do things they usually wouldn't because it's using words to stimulate hearts and minds. I know some people don't read books, and others, probably like our MP, don't believe reading fiction has value. But it does have value. It's not just some dalliance. I know this because only a tiny fraction of people get no joy out of reading. As a species, we seem to need it. It brings joy, without which it's just eat, fuck, work, and die, isn't it? Art is the extra stuff that makes the work part bearable. It's a big part of our existence, but we devalue those who do it for a living.' She glanced at the contents of the street library. 'Books of brilliant things, that's what I call them.'

The woman had a smile wide enough to consume the sun. 'I like you, lady, especially the swearing. What's your name?'

'Joanna.'

'Do people call you Jo?'

'I don't talk to many people.'

'Okay, Joanna, I'm Grace.' She offered Joanna the spell book. 'You take this, and I'll try that cooking hardback. I've been trying for years to find the perfect recipe for a spicy Moroccan carrot salad.' She grasped the book with her wrinkled fingers. 'And I'll see you back here at the same time in three days. Yes?'

Joanna nodded, then watched Grace wander towards the station.

Perhaps she arrived here on a ghost train.

Her mother had constantly ridiculed Joanna for believing in the supernatural. However, even though she'd matured out of childish things, and had read *The God Delusion* four times, she still had a lingering suspicion in the back of her mind there were unseen things all around her.

At university, she heard rumours of students dabbling with Ouija boards, of kids trying to summon the ghosts of the supposedly haunted buildings and of the lad who wanted a demon to help him pass his exams. In the end, she guessed, it had all been about booze, drugs, and sex, but there had been, for her, the odd occasion when she thought she'd seen something otherworldly from the corner of her eye.

'Eyes don't have corners,' her mother had said over the phone on the prison hotline. 'But your grandmother was a witch, so it might be in your blood.'

She carried that image back to the flat, fumbling with her keys as she tried to unlock the door. Joanna could feel a presence behind her, and she turned to see her neighbour standing just a few feet away. He was creepy-looking, with greasy hair and a sinister smile stretching from ear to ear. His eyes were dark and small, like a pair of shiny black beads, and they seemed to peer through her.

'Can I help you, Alan?'

'More books, Joanna?'

The tome was heavy in her hands. 'You can never have enough.'

He took a step closer and leaned in, his breath hot and foul on her face. 'Witches, eh? You better watch out, or there'll be another witch-hunt around here.'

Joanna had limited experiences with the internet and social media – not owning a mobile phone or television, the Devil's vomit in a box her mother used to call it – but she knew enough about online trolls attacking women to know that witch-hunts were a deeply upsetting modern thing. But she didn't think he was talking about those.

'There were witch-hunts around here?'

He scratched at his chin, and she noticed the blood under his nails. 'Oh, aye, there was. I'm no historian, but a bloke in the pub told me about this group of women tried for witchcraft in the sixteenth century.'

'What happened?'

Alan shrugged. 'I guess somebody accused them of consorting with the Devil.' She noticed his nicotine-stained teeth as he grinned. 'God knows what they'd say if they saw what today's girls get up to.' He leered at her, and she pulled back. 'We could read that together if you like.'

Joanna shook her head as she pushed the door open. 'Maybe some other time.'

She slammed the door behind her, already regretting telling him that. Now he'd think there was a chance in the future. Then she opened the spell book and a bottle of wine in that order.

And she read.

She returned to the street library three days later, waiting for Grace. There had been one close call with Alan, but she'd made the excuse of saying she might have Covid, and he scuttled off like a crab, muttering about vaccinations used by the government for mind control and tracking. She was glad she kept a stock of masks in the flat and would wear one whenever he was nearby.

She checked the books while waiting, seeing the collection of Philip K. Dick paperbacks, a coverless copy of a David Bowie biography, and a set of E. L. James novels.

'How come nobody has written a book called *Fifty Shades of Gay*? I'd read that in a heartbeat,' Grace said when she arrived. 'What a cabinet of curiosities that would be.'

'What have you got there?' Joanna said.

Grace held the book up. '*Lulu In Hollywood*. You know of Louise Brooks?'

Joanna shook her head. 'No.'

Grace laughed. 'Philistine.' She pointed at Joanna's hands. 'You've read the spell book already?'

'Yes, but it's much more than spells and incantations.'

'What do you mean?'

The wind whistled through Joanna's hair, the sound of an approaching train growing louder with each passing moment. She took a deep breath, letting the breeze wash over her as it blew her hair back from her face.

'There was a lot of history in the book I hadn't seen or read before regarding witches and witchcraft.'

The train howled as it sped towards the station. 'Go on,' Grace said.

Joanna thought of the ghost train as she watched the passengers step onto the platform.

'Well, it includes the theory that medieval witches had worshipped not a male Devil, but a female goddess; this and other features of their worship suggested it had originated in Neolithic times, before the rise of Patriarchy. So essentially, the ideas of witchcraft and witches are associated with women, yet, the further we return to early Christianity and pre-Christianity, the less is the stigma attached to the witch. It was only at the commencement of the fourteenth century that witchcraft was finally associated with heresy. These two imputations rolled into one and became a dominant instrument of oppression wielded by an all-powerful Church or a deadly but often double-edged weapon of revenge in the hands of private individuals.'

Grace nodded. 'We are the ghosts at the edge of the photographs, a history of our invisible names.'

Her words seeped into Joanna's brain as a train pulled into the station, the sound of its wheels grinding against the tracks. People crowded the platform, all waiting anxiously to board. The conductor leaned out the window, shouting the station's name as the train halted. The carriage doors opened with a hiss, and the public spilled out, eager to reach their destination. Footsteps and voices filled the air as the crowd made their way to the exit, some stopping to say goodbye to friends and loved ones who were staying behind. The train's horn signalled it was time to leave, and people rushed to find seats. The platform was a hive of activity, the sound of the train adding to the din of the busy station.

Perhaps it was a soul train, not like the Stevie Wonder song, but transport for those ready for the next world. Maybe that was why the street library was in that spot, a way of attracting lost souls and helping them on their journey. And Joanna was nothing if not a lost soul, as her mother regularly told her.

Joanna peered at the passengers, surprised at how many there were, much more than she'd seen before. She studied Grace, witnessing a shimmer around her long white hair.

'You don't seem surprised by what I said.'

'I'm not,' Grace said. 'In 1893, the American Matilda Joslyn Gage, in her *Woman, Church and State*, took a line still popular with feminists, that witches had been wise women and healers persecuted by a misogynist Church jealous of female power. Gage demonstrated how organisations and individuals use religious doctrine to justify depriving women of civil, human, economic and political rights, even denying women the right to worship alongside men.'

Joanna watched the train leave the station, staring at the ghostly faces in the windows.

'It's fascinating stuff.' She turned to Grace. 'Did you know there was a witch trial here five hundred years ago?'

Grace laughed. 'I'd hardly call it a trial. Twelve women were accused and brought to the town hall, publicly stripped and pricked with a pin to identify whether they were a witch. A witch was said to have a devil's mark on their body, where they couldn't feel any pain. Those accused had their clothes removed, and their bodies searched for one of these devil's marks, which were then pricked. They were undoubtedly a witch if they didn't bleed or couldn't feel anything, an invasive and implicitly sexualised method of trying the accused that would inevitably shame them, no matter the outcome.'

'What was the outcome?'

'The witch-finder condemned them to execution after he identified them as witches. The witch-finder's name was lost to history, but I discovered it while researching the village.'

'What was it?'

Grace moved closer to her. 'It was the ancestor of our local MP.'

Joanna placed a hand over her heart. 'The one who wants to remove the street library?'

'Indeed.' Her eyes sparkled as she gazed deep into Joanna. 'How will you survive without it?'

Joanna's lips trembled. 'Well, I did before.'

Grace shook her head. 'That was when your daily fuel

was a motley read of thrillers, kid's stories, and fake history. Since then, you've discovered the marvels of Leena Krohn, Joris-Karl Huysmans, *Alphabetical Africa*, Samuel Beckett, Gemma Files, Italo Calvino and Tanith Lee.'

'That's true, but can't I get those and others like them elsewhere?'

'Did you before?'

Joanna's heart thumped against her ribs. 'No.'

'So, you see, there's only one way out of this for you.'

'What?'

'You must place a curse on the man who wants to remove the most important thing from you.'

'A curse?'

Grace pointed at the spell book. 'Yes. Turn the tide against those who demonise anything that isn't them.' She touched Joanna's shoulder. 'Don't you see? This is all fate.'

Somewhere in the distance, Joanna heard the train screeching down the track. 'What do you mean?'

'The lines that tether us to the past are always with us. First, the witch-finder persecuted those poor women, and now his descendant wants to make things worse for you and many others. Finding those spells here was no accident. Don't you see that?'

I clasped the book to my chest. 'It wasn't?'

Grace shook her head. 'There's no such thing as coincidence, Joanna.' She placed a hand on the cover. 'It doesn't have to be one of the worst curses – unless that's what you want – just something to protect your street library.'

'But,' Joanna said. 'I don't even know what he looks like. I don't have a TV, phone, or computer, and I never read the newspapers.'

Grace grinned. 'If you had to create an image of him in your mind, he'd be someone wearing a mask, a flat hat and a striped jersey and carrying a bag marked SWAG. This is the name of his ancestor and the spell you must use.' She pushed her face into Joanna's and whispered the words. 'Do you know what to do?'

Joanna inched back from her, feeling more alive than she ever had. 'Of course.' Grace turned to leave. 'Wait,' Joanna said.

'What?'

'What was the book you took from the street library?'

Grace removed the tatty paperback from 'her pocket. 'This? I'll let you have it after you do what you must.'

Joanna read the title. '*The Day of Be-With-Us*. What's it about?'

Grace's laugh blended in with the scream of an approaching train. 'Everything, Joanna. It's about everything.'

Joanna watched her leave as the rain fell.

And she felt the power in her hands.

Lost in Music

I wasn't surprised to be the only one at my father's funeral. On the rare occasions when he spoke to me, from birth to the last time I saw him two years ago, he admitted he'd have to pay for people to turn up for him going out in a blaze of non-glory.

The ceremony finished inside twenty minutes, just me and the crematorium staff standing silently as the coffin wheeled away behind closed doors and into the furnace. The air smelt of roses and lavender, something far sweeter than the old man deserved. The staff stared at me, maybe expecting a final flurry of tears and sobs, but they received nothing in return. His presence felt like an absence, ninety-two years for him and fifty-four for me, and I was glad to be free of him.

Only it wasn't over; there was still the property to deal with. The family home was a twenty-minute ride from the cemetery, giving me enough time to drive there and finish two cigarettes. I had another one while I stood outside the house and stared at the building. The front garden looked immaculate; the old man's fingers were always more nurturing to the plants than his family. I guess the grass was greener on that side.

Why was I there? I'd arranged with the removal firm to come tomorrow and empty the place, and I didn't care what they did with the contents. I wanted nothing, no memories I desired to rekindle with a trip down that well-forgotten lane. And yet, I still entered.

The key creaked as I twisted it in the lock, placing my foot inside before I changed my mind. I kept my head down, went upstairs and into my childhood bedroom. When I lifted my eyes, it was as if I'd stepped back in time. The sheets on the bed were the same, and on the walls hung bright posters of my favourite movies and music. I ran my fingers over a crinkled copy of the poster for *Blade Runner*, the tiny tears in the paper dredging up memories of a person I hadn't been for years.

My legs wobbled, and I stopped, my hands reaching for the cupboard in search of ancient mementoes. I spun and left my youth behind me, bounding down the stairs and towards the front door. My hand grasped for the handle when something called to me from the living room, an echo of my name resonating down the decades.

My arm ached as I pushed inside. I glanced around, taking in the TV, three-piece suite, bookcase, and writing desk. My curiosity was sated, ready to leave, when I noticed something which surprised me: at the far end, near the chair he always sat in, stood the music centre my parents had bought me for my fourteenth birthday.

And it was switched on.

The red power light flickered at me. I reached for the nape of my neck and cursed the electricity company for not switching off the supply like they promised they would. Dust swirled in the air and up my nose as I moved to turn it off, my legs immobilised by the sight of the envelope sitting on top, the envelope with my name on it written in my father's handwriting. My throat shrivelled up as I coughed and spat onto the floor, the taste of wretched nostalgia lingering on my lips.

I took a step back and two deep breaths. I expected no monetary legacy from him; the sale of the house would pay off his gambling debts, but to think he'd left me a note made the breakfast I'd eaten that morning turn volcanic inside my gut.

The key dug into my palm, my chance to leave disappearing as I moved forward, picked up the envelope, and realised the weight and shape of the contents meant it could only be one thing.

A cassette.

I couldn't remember the last time I'd used one as I emptied it into my hand. It was an ACME Brand Type II Chrome 60 Minute Blank, and written on the side in that familiar printed writing were the words:

PLAY ME NOW, ANTHONY

The electricity slipped up my legs, sped through my chest, made my arms wobble, and thumped the back of my head. The tape fell from my fingers and clattered across the carpet. A spasm stung my body as I stumbled backwards and tumbled into the three-piece sofa. The cassette lay on the rug, the text burning an image across my retinas.

PLAY ME NOW, ANTHONY

He was the only one to call me that; even my teachers addressed me as Tony. My mother hated the name Anthony, and I'd never taken to it. I was Tony when I joined the army, Tony when the bomb blew up in front of me, Tony when I returned to civvy street, and Tony when my wife left me. Yet, as I sat in this room, I became Anthony all over again.

I reached down and grabbed the cassette, still on my knees, as I crawled towards the music player and opened the tape deck. I dropped it in, pressed play and stared at the speakers, waiting to hear his words chastise me one more time; instead, all I got was a wail of noise. It took me thirty seconds to realise it was a voice played backwards and another ten to notice the machine chewing up the cassette. I lunged forward and stopped it.

I ejected the contents from the player, making sure I removed it without causing more damage. It wasn't split or torn, just untangled from the spools. I grabbed a pencil and inserted the end into one spool, using it to rewind the tape into place. It trembled between my fingers when someone spoke.

'I never thought this would work.'

It was a sound I hadn't heard for two years, a voice belonging to a dead man. My head twisted as my knees pressed into the carpet. I wanted to get up but lacked the strength. He grinned at me, sparkling white teeth in a face much younger than his ninety-two years.

'You're dead.' I didn't know what else to say.

His grin expanded. 'Well, I was until you played that tape, son.'

He stepped forward and held out his hand. I scuttled back and into the music centre, the buttons on the tape player digging into me.

'I'm dreaming, aren't I?'

He glanced out the window and laughed. 'I made a deal with the Devil.'

'I saw you in the coffin, watched it seared by the flames in the crematorium. None of this is real.'

He ignored me and picked up the tape. 'Oh, it's real, Anthony. There's a bit of magic on this cassette, wound backwards, and released once you played it. That was the first part of the deal.' He placed it into his jacket pocket and sat down next to my trembling form. I scampered off the floor, got up, and stumbled for the door. Something hard and invisible smacked me in the face and sent me flying into the sofa.

'What the…?'

'Son, the Devil has to get something in return for resurrecting me.'

'Talk sense, old man.' I sat up and glared at him.

'It's simple, Anthony. I swapped your soul for mine. I'm fifty-four again.' He flexed his fingers as if using them for the first time. 'I'd wanted to die sooner, to become you when you were younger, but I had to let nature run its course. That was the most important condition of the deal.'

'What do you mean, become me?'

'You're stuck in here until she arrives to collect you, but once I leave, I'll be in your body, living your life.' He raised a hand to his face and peered at the lines on the flesh. 'Fifty-four isn't great, but it's better than ninety-two and preferable to being dead.' He rose from the chair. 'Now, I should go before she comes.'

I shook my head and laughed. 'You can't sell my soul without my permission.'

He grinned again. 'Finally, you're coming to your senses.' He reached into his jacket and removed a piece of paper. 'Do you remember your sixteenth birthday when I took out an insurance policy for you?'

I sneered at him. 'I recollect you telling me you cashed it in two years later so you could pay off your debts.'

'That was a ruse, boy.' He held the paper out, revealing the writing on the bottom. 'Do you recall signing this?'

My heart shrivelled as I sank into the chair. He returned the contract to his pocket and walked past me. His hand reached for the door as he turned; there were no more words, just that bright, annoying grin. He left the house before I could reply. I stood and stared through the window, watching as someone who looked like me strode away.

'Everything he told you is true.'

I froze to the spot as she appeared, my eyes turning towards her. My lips shook as I spoke.

'Are you the De...?'

She held out her hand. 'I'm Lucy, your employer.'

I took her fingers without thinking; her skin was warm, and she smelt of jasmine.

'Employer?'

'I need a new Reaper, and I think you'd be perfect for the job. With all your experience with death, I think you'll enjoy collecting your first soul.'

We stared out the window together. 'Collecting a soul?'

'You kept one last secret from your father, didn't you, Tony?' She was still holding my fingers.

My breath chilled the glass. 'It's why I went to the funeral.'

Her voice sang like the low hum of a violin. 'How long did the doctors give you?'

'About a week.'

'And when was this?'

'Six days ago.'

Lucy let go of my hand and put her arm around my shoulder. 'Yes, I think you'll enjoy your new job, Tony.' Then she peered out the window. 'And you'll love the first one.'

The Doll House

Mary Croft cancelled her *Fashion Doll Quarterly* magazine subscription the morning she murdered her husband. It was the most painful thing she'd ever done — the cancellation, not the murder.

She'd thought about killing him for ages. The first time was a week after their wedding, when she caught him sleeping with the bridesmaid.

'It's not what you think, Mary,' he'd said as he pushed the woman to the side so forcefully she fell out of bed, her arm and legs going in different directions. Mary saw enough to realise she wasn't a natural blonde.

Mary rubbed at the bruise below her cheek. Not one person at the wedding had mentioned the injury, and even the minister believed the story she'd spun about walking into the door. She assumed they were all whispering about how long her marriage to Harry Croft would last, but it wasn't her future husband who'd hit her, but the father she was desperate to escape. He didn't attend the ceremony, so Mary took that as an excellent start to her new life.

Harry's infidelity with the bridesmaid should have

warned her off the relationship, but she was prepared to put up with it as long as it got her away from *him*.

But thirty years of lies and deceit finally snapped her patience. That's why Harry was upstairs with a blade in the neck and a wound in his gut for each year of their marriage. She peered at the blood on her hands, inhaling the smell of burnt copper as she went to the kitchen. Mary gazed at the recently bought cutlery rack.

'It looks uneven without the largest bread knife.'

She ran her fingers under warm water, wondering if she should leave Harry where he was. She dried her hands and opened the fridge, pouring herself a large glass of white wine. It tasted sweet as the anxiety eased out of her shoulders, and she relaxed for the first time in ages. She retreated to the living room and retrieved her book, flicking through the pages of Stephen King's *The Stand*. Mary had read it more than once, always fixated on what her life would have been like if a pandemic had spread across the globe and wiped out most of the population.

'The world would have been a better place, that's for sure, without humanity destroying the climate.'

Several times she'd tried to get Harry to buy an electric car and reduce his meat consumption, but he'd always refused.

'It's all fake news, Mary, spread by loony left-wingers wanting to steal the good things in life from people like us.'

People like us.

Not for the first time, she'd wondered why she'd married him. And not for the first time, she'd come back with the same answer: to get away from *him*.

She finished the glass of wine and put the book down, her mind feeling fuzzy and unfocused. Mary was fifty years old, and now Harry was dead, there was only one person left she truly hated. Her father had died last year — she'd celebrated far too much when that happened, getting a stinking hangover that had lasted the whole day after the funeral. Harry didn't care since he was off with his scarlet woman, only returning home as Mary threw up in the garden pond, spitting spew all over his precious tropical fish.

'England's climate wasn't made for green and orange fish,' she told him as he dredged the contents of her guts from the water.

He never said a word or gave her a dirty look, and she knew why. Because if he'd mentioned it, she would have had the perfect excuse to ask him where he'd been all night, even if Mary had known he was with her. She'd always known where he was: when your husband was screwing your best friend for thirty years, she'd needed to have been some kind of stupid not to know what was happening.

Mary didn't remember ever being truly happy in her life. There may have been times as a young child before her mother ran away and her father took out his failures on her, but she couldn't recall them.

'You're a sturdy girl, Mary,' her teachers told her. 'Nothing spectacular, but neither are you one of those girls who'll go off the rails and hang around with the wrong crowd.'

She poured another glass of wine, regretting she'd never fallen in with the wrong people. Her neck ached as she peered at the ceiling, sighing because it had taken her so long to do something so wrong but had felt so right.

Mary stared into the mirror next to her precious doll collection. It was Harry's idea to hang a mirror there even though she'd argued against it. She hated her reflection, looking at eyes that were too small and a nose that was too big. It wasn't their size that bothered her, but the fact they reminded her too much of *him*.

Before her face turned into *him*, she moved from her echo and went to her collection. The dolls made her smile. Some of Mary's fondest childhood memories were about playing with them. So while she didn't walk them through a pretend house anymore, she displayed and changed them around, finding new details on many she hadn't noticed or appreciated before. Those dolls listened to her complaints, accepted her, and embraced her. They were quiet and loyal, keeping her company on those nights when her loneliness had threatened to overwhelm her.

At first, Harry hated her collection. Early in her marriage, she'd thought he would destroy the dolls, but as time passed, he ignored them, leaving her with them so she spent more time with them than with him. It was only later that she understood he was doing this so he could frolic with his other woman.

'Come upstairs, Mary, and lie with me.'

She heard Harry's voice but knew it was only in her head. Even if he was still alive, which he wasn't with those thirty stab wounds in his stomach, she'd sliced his throat so deeply it had filled with blood, making it impossible to speak. Instead, he'd stumbled around the room, bumping into furniture and knocking several dolls she kept near the bed across the floor. Mary had watched him bleed all over her rare Rita Hayworth doll, gasped when he stood on and crushed Marilyn Monroe's face, and shed a tear when her husband collapsed in a heap on top of Brigitte Bardot's porcelain chest.

'I wonder if I can claim on the insurance?' she'd said as Harry clutched at the kitchen knife sticking out of his throat.

He wriggled on the carpet for a few minutes before stopping, and she went downstairs and left him there. Mary thought again of how she'd never see her collection after today. She'd started it after her mother had fled the family home, her only escape from life until her marriage, when she thought she wouldn't need her dolls anymore. Now she'd have a real person to love her, she believed. But it never worked out like that.

She licked a stray bit of blood from the top of her finger, mixing it with the taste of the wine. Her stomach rumbled, and she realised she hadn't eaten breakfast.

Then the doorbell rang.

Mary got up and went to the door, opening it and smiling at the person who stood there. Annie Clark's eyes were as big as a frog's, her mouth so wide she looked like she was auditioning for a porn film, which was appropriate. She'd travelled so far in thirty years, a bridesmaid no more.

'Surprised to see me, Annie?'

'No.... no, Mary. I just thought you'd be at the hospital this morning. So I came to drop something off for you.'

Mary moved aside. 'You better come in, then.'

Annie stepped inside, and Mary led her into the living room, where she stared at the half-empty bottle of wine.

'Should you be drinking in....'

Mary grabbed the bottle. 'In my condition?'

Annie nodded. 'Harry told me the bad news.'

'He told you the hospital doesn't have a donor for a kidney transplant?'

'Yes. I'm sorry, Mary.'

She waved the wine at Annie. 'Would you like a drink to celebrate?'

Annie shook her head. 'Can I have a glass of water?'

Mary laughed. 'Of course. You sit down, and I'll get us both one.'

She went to the kitchen, singing a silent song inside her head as she prepared the drinks. Annie was on the sofa when she returned. Mary handed her the water, and she downed it in one go.

'Why would I be celebrating?'

Mary sat opposite her. 'Come on, Annie, there's no need to lie anymore. I know you've been shagging my husband for the last thirty years. Now I've only got a few months to live, and you can have him all to yourself.'

Annie Clark gulped and rubbed her throat. Mary watched her struggle for a reply.

'You should never have married him.'

It wasn't the reply Mary had expected.

'Did you pretend to be my friend all this time, Annie, so you could stay close to him?'

'We only want what's best for you, Mary.'

Mary nearly choked on her laughter, glancing at the stairs and remembering what was up there.

'Well, Annie, I don't know how to thank you for that. Perhaps you should go to our bedroom where Harry is waiting for you.' She finished the glass of water. 'I assume you know where it is.'

Annie Clark jumped out of her seat and ran upstairs. Mary waited for the scream, grinning when it arrived thirty seconds later, followed by the wailing and tears. She'd returned to the wine by the time her friend came back downstairs.

'What have you done, Mary?'

Annie slumped onto the sofa and grasped at her throat.

'Do you mean about Harry, or are you talking about the arsenic I put in your water?' She smiled at the former bridesmaid. 'How fitting we'll both perish because of kidney failure, though I'll last longer than you.'

She raised her glass in a toast as Annie clasped at her jacket, reaching inside for something.

'I've already called the police, so you don't need your phone.'

But it wasn't a mobile she got as her eyes glazed over, clutching a piece of paper as her head slumped into the pillow with Frida Kahlo's face on it. Mary put her drink down and grabbed the paper. She heard the sirens approaching as she read it aloud.

'Dear Ms Clark, I'm happy to confirm that you are a match as a kidney donor for Mrs Croft. I want to arrange for the two of you to come and see me as soon as possible. Yours sincerely, Dr Thomas Marx.'

The paper trembled in Mary's fingers as the doorbell rang.

Then Mary Croft stared at her broken dolls.

'Shit!'

Sid Vicious in the Attic

Donna Bird was alone on her sixtieth birthday when she discovered her husband was a serial killer.

She climbed into the attic to store the week's local newspapers and magazines when the ache in her head returned. Her legs throbbed as she sat on a box of old records and sneezed. Donna wiped the snot from her nose on her cardigan sleeve, noticing how Ruffles the cat judged her through its glittering green eyes. She reached into her pocket and removed the bottle of pills. Her throbbing skull signalled what would follow since quitting the tablets three days ago.

'Have you taken your medication?' Robert, her husband, used to say twice a day. But he'd stopped caring a long time ago. About that, anyway. He was still angry about her junk in the attic.

'Why do you collect all this rubbish?' he said once, after picking up a dusty newspaper from fifty years ago. It had been printed on Donna's birthday, but he never noticed. 'If you're going to save stuff, why not get things that might be valuable?' He threw the paper back into the pile. 'You can sell anything online these days, but not your garbage.'

Donna had never dared tell him that she only collected what the voices in her head told her to. And those voices had been with her for a very long time. Longer than he'd been with her.

But they'd stopped once she'd started on the pills. She hadn't wanted to visit the doctor – Robert had insisted – knowing the quack would take one look at her before scribbling one of those notes keeping the pharmaceutical industry wealthy. Still, she'd got one useful thing from the trip to the GP, staring at the bunch of magazines stolen from the surgery.

She ran her fingers over the magazine covers with their beautiful models proclaiming that *you too, could look this good*. Of course, it was all nonsense, but somebody must have believed it since these women's periodicals were more popular than cheap gin and frozen pizzas. Lurid headlines screamed at her: *My Lover Is A Ghost*; *I Married My Dog*, and Donna's favourite – *I Buried My Dad Under The Rose Bushes*.

After her marriage, she perused such magazines in the vain hope they'd tell her how to be a perfect wife. There had been advice on clothes to buy and wear, though they never worked for her. She'd once bought a red dress made popular by a member of the Royal Family, who Donna admitted had looked fabulous in it, but it had only turned her into a ruby potato. The magazine experts had shown her how to apply the right makeup, but none of it could fix her face. She'd read many tips on improving her culinary abilities, and there were always plenty of instructions on how to please your man in the bedroom. But there had been no pleasing Robert, especially where sex was concerned.

The thought of *that* sent an explosion shooting through her skull.

Donna ignored the pain in her head, smiled at the cat, and went to the favourite part of her hobby – the records she'd collected in the 70s. She'd never told Robert there were valuable discs in the collection: the picture disc of The Clash's *Straight to Hell*; *Reality Asylum* by Crass; The Damned's *Don't Cry Wolf* on pink vinyl; The Dickies *Eve of Destruction* with the misprinted sleeve; and a promotional copy of The Only Ones *Another Girl, Another Planet*.

She touched the sleeves, the images resurrecting the happiest times of her youth when Donna had found something to ease her loneliness. It didn't matter then that the other girls laughed and pointed at her or that they criticised her musical tastes because she knew that the music and the lyrics were much more important to her than being close to another human being. People had always let her down. That was until she met Robert.

It was one thing they had bonded over after they stumbled into each other at a Sisters of Mercy gig, their shared love of music. His hair was as ebony and spiky as hers, and their combined dark clothing made them resemble a black hole when they got together. But over the years, their musical tastes had drifted apart as they had. She still listened to punk and goth songs, but he was more into Adele and Ed Sheeran. She was glad because it meant spending less time with him and she didn't have to suffer through his rants against immigrants, lefties, and the Woke. He wasn't so intolerant when they'd met, and she couldn't understand how he'd changed so much.

'You know why, Donna.'

She didn't look up at the sound of the voice she hadn't

heard for so long. Instead, her fingers gripped the bottle of pills, the rattle unable to stop him from speaking again.

'You shouldn't be here,' she said. 'Robert won't like it.'

And her doctor wouldn't.

'Robert lost his job and blamed foreigners because the media told him to. And whenever he sees a gay person in TV shows or movies, it reminds him of the thoughts buried deep in his unconscious. Only they aren't buried, and he has to distract himself from them by doing terrible things.'

Donna lifted her head. 'What terrible things?'

The man in tight leather trousers and a hairstyle created by Edward Scissorhands moved towards her.

'It's all in here, Donna, in this attic. This is where he keeps his trophies. He's much more vicious than I ever was.'

She smiled at her old friend. 'You weren't vicious, Sidney. You were just misunderstood.'

His lips curled up into that sneer that always made her go weak at the knees.

'Johnny named me after his hamster, so I couldn't have been all bad, could I?'

She didn't want to talk about the things he'd done.

'Why have you come back to me, Sidney?'

Donna heard his bones creak as he bent next to her.

'You know why. Last time you were in the attic, you saw what he keeps here.' He pointed at the pills. 'They made you forget, but you're better now. You have to stop him from hurting anybody else.'

She listened to his words, knowing they weren't his but her subconscious telling her what she'd read from her husband's mind.

Such terrible, terrible things. Worse than anything she'd seen before.

Donna was a teenager when she realised the voices in

her head were other people's thoughts. She tried to drown them out but had to look elsewhere for help when they transformed into visions. Loud music helped at first, but as she got older, her ability grew stronger, so she reached for other crutches: alcohol, drugs and sex. Until eventually, only the state-prescribed medication could do the trick.

But those pills had robbed her of who she really was and turned her into a walking vegetable capable of doing only the simplest things.

'Why did you stop taking the tablets, Donna?' the spiky-haired vision said.

'I saw you again; only it wasn't you. There's a TV drama about you and the others, and I watched an actor playing you. I knew then it was a message to regain control of my life. That's when I quit the pills.'

He smiled at her. 'And here we are now.'

Donna nodded, understanding what he wanted her to do, realising what she needed to do. She got up and moved past the magazines and seven-inch singles to the back of the attic. She placed one hand on the large antique chest standing against the wall. It had been her mother's and her mother's mother's. Both women had ended their lives in institutions that had done them more harm than good.

I got my abilities from them.

She ran her fingers over the wood, touching the rusty metal clasp.

I don't want to open it.

Even though she understood what was inside.

The old punk sat next to her. 'You have to stop him, Donna, before he kills again.'

The Slasher, that's what the media called him. The maniac who'd butchered at least six women. She knew he'd also done other dreadful things to them, but she never read or listened to those details.

Donna's heart resembled a broken window as she lifted the lid of the chest, her eyes widening as she stared at her mother and grandmother's old dresses. She touched the top dress, a vibrant red ball gown smelling of innocence and better times.

I could just stay like this. I don't have to go any further.

She felt Sidney's ghostly touch on her arm and pictured her freckles spinning like dust caught in the wind. She removed all the clothes she recognised until she came to the bits she didn't: jewellery, underwear, socks and even an expensive watch. She'd seen the watch before, on the news. It had belonged to the first victim. In her mind, after she'd stopped taking the pills, she'd watched Robert tear it from the woman's wrist. The screams had filled her mind for days, the pain turning her body to stone.

All I have to do is call the police.

Sidney shook his head. 'We don't trust the police, Donna, remember?'

She did. When she was a teenager, two drunks attacked her. They'd clawed at her and tried to rip her clothes off until she'd stumbled away and grabbed a large piece of wood from the ground, using it to crack the skull of the first one and shatter the jaw of the other. The police charged her with GBH, and she spent nine months in jail.

'You still have a police record.' He grinned at her. 'And I don't mean that terrible *Walking on the Moon* song.'

She laughed and wiped a tear from her eye. 'So what should I do?'

'You're not the only collector in the house, Donna.'

She flinched at his words, twisting around to see Robert

grinning at her. She grabbed her mother's clothes, bringing them close to her as protection.

'I was thinking of taking some of my things to the charity shop.' Something cold grasped at her chest. 'You're always saying I should get rid of this stuff, and you're right.'

Her husband crept towards her, and she noticed the kitchen knife in his hand.

'You've always been a terrible liar, Donna.' He pointed the blade at her. 'Do you lie to the voices in your head?'

She moved backwards like a crab and pushed her spine into the wall.

'What do you mean?'

His grin increased until it filled most of his face.

'I know you've stopped taking your pills. And that means you'll have the voices in your head again. Do you see things as well?'

She peered at Robert and glanced at Sidney standing next to him. Sid reached out a ghostly hand and ran it over her husband's throat.

'I haven't seen anything.'

Robert shook his head. 'Yes, you have, Donna. You've been admiring my collection in that box.'

The words crawled over her lips. 'Your collection?'

He nodded. 'Yes, all the souvenirs I took from those women I killed.'

She pushed harder against the wall, wishing it would swallow her whole.

'You're the Slasher?'

Robert held out his arms and bowed to her. 'I am. So what are you going to do about it?'

'I'll call the police.'

He waved the blade at her. 'Who do you think they'll believe? A nutcase who hears voices or a respected local community member and hard-working accountant employed by the council.' He nodded at the chest. 'I'll hide that somewhere else, and once they dig into your criminal past, they'll lock you up for your terrible lies. And then someone will leak the story all over social media. Mad Donna, that's what they'll call you. Your life will be hell.'

She dug her nails into her palm, feeling the blood trickle over her skin.

'My life has been hell for a long time, Robert.'

He moved closer to her. 'You've loved every minute of it.' He rubbed his sweaty hand over her cheek. 'You like the pain and the humiliation, don't you? I recognised it in you the first time we met. That's why I chose you as my facade, the other half of me, to project the illusion of respectability and conformity to the world.' He ran his fingers through her hair, and she stopped herself from throwing up. 'You've been a good stooge, Donna. I couldn't have picked anybody better.'

Donna's eyes were like lead weights. 'I thought you loved me. In the beginning, at least.'

Robert flicked the knife between his hands. 'You were a mess, but one I could sculpt to my own ends. You had no friends, and with the money your parents had left you, it was perfect. Fate brought us together, don't you see? Predator and victim coexisting in pure symbiosis.' He laughed at her. 'It's why marriage was invented.'

She avoided the darkness in his eyes and glanced at the chest. 'The things you took from the women you killed. Why did you hide them under those clothes?'

He stood up and beamed at her. 'I didn't hide them, Donna. I wanted you to find them.'

A chill ran down her face and into her heart. 'Why?'

'Why? Because I needed you to understand who I really

am, what I'm capable of. I wanted you to know who you've been married to all this time. And I required you to recognise that you're stuck with me for the rest of your miserable life, and there's nothing you can do about it.'

'You're not going to kill me?'

His laugh disturbed the dust in the rafters, so it fell around her like grey confetti.

'Kill you? Of course not. You're what I show to the outside world, the perfect mirage. So why would I get rid of that?'

'I could still go to the police.'

Sidney and Robert shook their heads simultaneously.

'You won't,' Robert said. 'You don't have that type of courage.'

The phantom punk whispered in her ear. 'You do, Donna. You always have.'

'What do you mean?' she said.

Robert kicked her box of records. They tumbled onto the floor and the cat scampered out of the attic.

'You're a coward.'

'No,' Sidney said. 'He's wrong.' He pointed at the collection of seven-inch singles sprawled around her. 'All you need is the music to realise your full potential, Donna. Make them play.'

'What?'

Robert snarled at her. 'You heard me.'

Sidney's touch was warm on her face. 'You read minds, Donna. You always have. When your parents called you crazy, when you thought you heard voices, you were reading their thoughts. You tried your best to understand this ability, turning others' thoughts into the voices you recognised from your records. Eventually, you attached a comforting figure to the sounds.'

'You?' she whispered.

'Yes, dear old Sidney. But you've always been more than telepathic, Donna. You're a telekinetic as well.'

'What does that mean?'

He gazed into her eyes. 'Remember when you used your mind to smash those plates in your parent's kitchen?' She nodded. 'And the time you threw the bully across the school playground just by looking at him?'

She did. 'Yes.'

'And when those men attacked you, and you defended yourself with that piece of wood?'

'I grabbed that from the ground.'

'No,' he said. 'It was too far away. So you used your mind to search for it, and then you bashed their heads in. That's telekinesis, Donna. You move things with your thoughts.' He pointed at the records. 'And you can make them play now.'

Robert was speaking to her, but she didn't hear the words. So instead, she focused on her seven-inch singles, gazing at them as if they were the music of the gods. And to her, they were.

One by one, they lifted from the floor, rising in the air like raindrops in reverse.

But she didn't know what to do next.

How do I get them to play?

'You know, Donna.'

It wasn't Sidney speaking, but another familiar voice. She looked up as they all stepped out of the shadows: Poly Styrene. Joe Strummer. Ian Curtis. Siouxsie Sioux. Hugh Cornwell. Dave Vanian. Ari Up.

They all came and more and told her what to do. The singles drifted out of their record sleeves and started spinning.

'What the fuck?' Robert said.

Then the music of her youth exploded around the attic.

No More Heroes played with *Germ Free Adolescents*, *London Calling*, and *Typical Girls*. They all mixed together and transported Donna to the time she'd loved so much.

Robert pointed the knife at her. 'What are you doing?'

She gazed at the blade. 'Something better change, Robert.'

With one flick of her mind, Donna turned his hand around and plunged the knife into his heart. He stumbled back and crashed to the floor, his wild cries unable to drown out the music in her head. She stood over her husband and watched him die before returning all the records to their sleeves. Then she went downstairs and opened Robert's laptop. It took her two minutes to type his confession and suicide note. She didn't print a copy. Then she rang the police. When that was over, she sat next to Sidney on the sofa.

'Well, Donna, this is the first day of the rest of your life. What will you do with it?'

She dropped the pills in the bin. 'I need a holiday in the sun.'

Paradise Found

It's hard to get lost when you don't know where you belong.

And now here I was, stuck on a tiny aeroplane, flying to one of the remotest parts of the UK. The pilot had grinned at me as I'd stepped on board, a startling sight as there were too many teeth in his mouth, like the creature in *Alien*. He smelt of mustard, and the stains on his uniform hadn't eased my worries about the flight.

Not that I was afraid of flying – having flown several times, accompanying my parents around the world as part of my father's demanding job – but the size of the plane, or lack of it, had frayed my nerves.

And then it got worse.

The plane jerked forwards, throwing me to the side as if I was on the dodgems at the funfair. My hands dug into the seat, and I broke a purple fingernail. The pilot told the passengers not to worry, but I could tell by their faces they didn't believe him. My parents were unconcerned – my father snored away while my mother scribbled in her notebook, likely writing one of her mysterious poems she refused to show anybody.

My nose twitched at the smell of something burning. I glanced around the narrow space, my head spinning inside a tumble dryer. The woman sitting opposite me smiled as the plane bounced through the clouds, and I wondered what she was so happy about. Then she gripped the crucifix at her throat and pushed it towards me as if she was a new mother showing off her child. I assumed she either believed that God would protect her or she'd soon be meeting Him on the other side. Neither thought made me feel any better.

My stomach churned as the taste of the awful food masquerading as a meal threatened to burst out of my guts. I ignored it and imagined the new life waiting for me down below. I glanced out of the window as the plane trembled again. But like Miss Havisham's wedding party, I refused to accept that it wouldn't happen. I'd been lonely in Berlin, but what was coming next would be much worse.

The shaking didn't last long, and the pilot took us into a descent as I pushed aside any thoughts of dragons guiding me to the airport. According to my father, I'm an adult now, and adults don't waste time on fantasy and imagination.

'You're sixteen, Clara, a grown-up. There's no time for childish things if you want to survive in this world,' he'd said before telling me we were moving home again. My mother had only nodded in agreement, always consenting to his every word.

The plane landed smoothly, and everybody sighed with relief. My father woke and rubbed the sleep from his eyes. My mother put away her notebook. Neither of them spoke to the other. Or me. But that was okay. I was used to it. As we stood, I glanced at her, knowing she'd never wanted a child but was doing her best. But, on the other hand, my father had craved a son, so I could be nothing more than the runners-up prize for him.

We stepped off the plane onto a beach, my feet sinking into the sand as the driving rain attempted to remove the skin from my face. I wiped the water from my eyes and stared at the surroundings: the sea was behind me, the torrent crashing into it as one long black sheet as if Poseidon's arm was reaching into the sky to grasp the hand of Zeus. Thankfully, thunder and lightning didn't follow as I focused on our destination, the main building making up Barra Airport.

My mother smiled as if we'd won the lottery. 'Welcome to Barradise.'

My father pulled up his coat to his face, leading us inside, my mother smiling as we stepped out of the cold and into the warmth. The other passengers headed for hot food and drinks from the café as I slumped into the nearest chair and dripped onto the floor. I heard the pilot mumbling behind me, complaining that he shouldn't have landed because there was too much water on the beach. Glancing into his eyes made me wonder how close we'd come to crashing.

We had one backpack each for our belongings since my father had sent the bulk of our stuff to the island before we arrived. I looked forward to sorting through my clothes and books when we got to the cottage, watching the passengers sip on hot tea as I licked water from my lips.

'We'll eat when we get to our accommodation,' my father said. 'The hire car should be on the other side of the building.'

That was our instruction to follow him through the airport. My mother lugged her bag over her shoulder as I took one last look at those who'd been on the plane, wondering if I'd see any of them again while I was on the Isle of Barra. Then I lifted my aching frame and grabbed my bag, scowling about the fingernail I'd lost.

Outside, the smell of isolation mingled with the water sticking to my face. At least the rain had stopped as I stuck out my tongue and tasted nature; there was nothing but grey skies and a bleak landscape before me.

'We'll be gone before winter arrives.'

There was zero concern in my father's voice. However long we'd be on Barra, his job would consume all his time, while my mother would lock herself away somewhere with her pen and paper, leaving me to my solitude.

That was the one thing I was looking forward to.

My father spotted the car, and we dumped our bags into the boot. I got into the back and stared at my phone, expecting no internet but always hopeful. It was hope that didn't last long. Instead, I plugged the headphones into the mobile and my ears, hitting the playlist I'd created before leaving for Barra. Billie Eilish serenaded me as we set off.

'The drive to the cottage should only take thirty minutes,' my father said. Peering out the window, I glimpsed the island through the gloom, seeing a landscape carved out of nature over thousands of years. Grey rock forms littered the land, jutting out from between the grass as if they'd been pushed up from beneath the earth's crust by some angry god. We drove past crags and rocks that could have represented some deserted alien planet on the far side of the universe. I glanced at my reflection in the glass, determined to make the most of this journey even though it wasn't as glamorous as our recent trips to Berlin and Vienna.

My mind drifted back to our time in Germany, of my struggles with the language and the other kids at the English school, when the car swerved to the side. I jerked up like a puppet and banged my head into the window. Pain shot through my cheek and into my jaw. The headphones fell from my ears as I heard the screech of the tyres and my father swearing. The wheels bounced off the narrow single-track and found the grass verge before returning to the road.

'Stupid idiot,' my father said as he tooted the horn at the car in the distance behind us.

My mother stared at me with tired eyes. 'Are you all right, Clara?'

I rubbed at my throbbing jaw and retrieved the headphones.

'I'm fine.'

My father grumbled as we drove, dodging the occasional wandering sheep. The coast was on my left, hills to my right, as we sped between the island's houses and buildings. It wasn't long before we reached our accommodation. Wet hair plastered my cheeks as I jumped out, following my mother to the cottage. She fumbled with the key in the door as I peered at a moving dark shadow above us. Then it swooped down at me. I staggered backwards into my father, his scowl as black as the bird that fluttered towards my face before it headed towards the silvery full moon filling the sky.

'I didn't know you feared birds, Clara.' His smile didn't make me feel any better. 'That raven seems to have taken a shine to you.'

My mother opened the door and dropped her bag on the carpet. 'Perhaps the raven was a descendent of Huginn or Muninn.'

The light from the doorway illuminated the surroundings as my heart continued to thump like a runaway train.

'What's a Huginn or Muninn?'

My father shook his head. 'Didn't you do your home-work about the island before leaving Germany?'

I shrugged. 'I thought I'd do it on the plane, but there was no internet connection.'

I glanced at the lack of bars on my mobile phone and guessed it would be a long time before I got online again.

'A head full of dreams, that's you, Clara,' my father said as he strode into the cottage.

I followed him inside and shut the door behind me. 'So, what's a Huginn or Muninn?'

We stepped into the living room as my mother answered.

'Huginn and Muninn are Odin's ravens from Norse mythology.' She narrowed her eyebrows and looked at me. 'You know who Odin was?'

My legs ached as I sat on a vivid red sofa. 'Of course. I've seen all the Thor movies.'

And I'd fantasised about Valkyrie.

A deep sigh drifted out of my father and settled across the room.

'What have I told you about putting away childish things, Clara?' He moved to the window and picked up the binoculars the cottage's owners had left behind, even though it was too dark to see what was outside. 'This island takes part of its name from Viking settlers, and it's said that ghostly warrior maidens can sometimes be seen chasing Odin's ravens in the dead of night.'

I scrutinised my father's face, searching for the twist of humour long missing in his demeanour. He was a dedicated man of science with no time for flights of fantasy or imagi-nation, but I couldn't tell if he was winding me up or not.

My mother's voice dragged me away from him. 'Your room is at the top of the stairs, Clara.'

She'd tried to show me photos of the place before we'd set off, but I'd had no interest. Yet now I was here, anticipation bubbled through my veins, and it was hard to keep my fingers from shaking. Perhaps I'd find books about Vikings and the Valkyrie here and have something to occupy my mind while my parents kept out of my way.

My mother returned to the car as the wind swept the rain into the house. I sprinted upstairs, searching for my room, a head full of romantic images and gothic visions of the past lives this building had witnessed. I threw open the door and dived onto the bed. Everything was white apart from the light blue cover. Nature whistled outside the window as I stared at the ceiling and contemplated where my exploration of the island would begin.

As I did so, I felt something digging into my spine. There was a large object under the bed. I rolled off it and dragged the covers up to discover a giant box. It took all my strength and both hands to pull it from its hiding place.

Tiny palpitations exploded in my heart at discovering this hidden thing, wondering about the secrets the previous occupants had left behind. I pulled the cardboard back and peered into the box. Someone had stacked hundreds of small pieces of paper on top of each other. When I thrust my hands inside, I realised they were photographs of different shapes and sizes. I took a handful and laid them in three rows on the floor, twelve in total, some in colour and others in black and white, but the subject was the same in every one of them: a beautiful young girl.

I gazed at the photos as I heard my parents unpacking the luggage downstairs. In my haste to get upstairs, I'd forgotten to bring my suitcase that was sent to the cottage ahead of us. My mother shouted something, but I didn't register what it was as I focused on what I'd found and returned to the images.

The girl looked like a teenager, maybe a few years older than me, and was the focus of every picture: shoulder-length dark hair, coal-fire brown eyes, and cheeks highlighted with a subtle dash of blush. I grabbed the largest image, and she peered out of it with arched red lips that appeared on the verge of talking to me. She was the most beautiful girl I'd ever seen. My fingers trembled so much that it was as if the photo's contents came alive, like animation in my hand. I could have sworn those ruby lips were whispering something to me.

My heart stopped racing, frozen against my ribs. I couldn't take my eyes away, knowing she was gazing deep inside me. It was as if all the great things in my life had been rolled into one: the first time I tasted ice cream; seeing Self Esteem play live; watching *Stranger Things* on Netflix; reading *Paper Girls*; hearing Billie Eilish; playing with the dog I could never have; staring out of a plane at the earth below me; swimming in a warm sea, and that rush I got when diving towards the ground on a rollercoaster.

I closed my eyes and counted to ten, imagining Odin's ravens whispering in my ear. Then I opened them and turned the picture over to find a single word on the back.

Julia.

I held it and stared at the others, settling on the smallest ones: three small black and white photos that looked like they'd been split from a passport ID. She smiled in one, grinned in another, and appeared gloomy in the third. I turned over all the images I'd removed from the box, and Julia's name was on the back of every one. I left them scattered on the floor, searching the rest of my bedroom, looking through the wardrobe and bookcase to see if there was anything else of her in the room, but found nothing. I peered under the bed again, finding only dust and cobwebs. Finally, dejected, I flopped onto the bed in frustration.

The photos lay on the carpet below me, but I couldn't look at them. That warm glow that had spread through me like a virus on seeing Julia in them was fading with the realisation I'd become infatuated with an image. The disappointment sank through me in waves, unnerving me in more ways than one. The instant fascination with some stranger in a bunch of photos was unlike me. I sat up and grabbed the box, emptying all the images over the bed, so they floated down slowly and reminded me of rainbow-coloured streamers at a carnival. There must have been hundreds of them.

I snatched one from the middle of the pile, a shiny Polaroid all beaten up around the edges. Julia was standing on the beach, the horizon behind her and birds swooning above, with that long hair billowing in the wind as she grinned at the photographer in her chic red and white striped dress. Her eyes mesmerised me, enchanted by that face.

Nobody else was in the photos, just Julia, at the house or around the island. Some had been taken in my new bedroom, others from inside the downstairs living room. Then there were the ones outside, highlighting spots on Barra I was determined to visit. Derelict buildings and rock-strewn ruins were the backgrounds to Julia's mesmerising eyes peering through the static images and into the living world: gazing into my world.

I placed my hands into the middle of the pile, feeling something large and sharp at the bottom: a compact disc. I didn't have a CD player. My father had a work laptop, but I wasn't allowed near that.

'Food is ready,' my mother shouted from downstairs.

I left the photos as they were, but put the CD under my pillow. Then, with an aching heart, I went down to sit with my parents, wondering what I would do with that treasure trove of pictures I'd discovered.

My mother placed a plate of hot soup in front of me. The smell of tomatoes rushed into my head and swam into my guts.

'How's your room, Clara?' she said.

I scooped a spoonful of soup into my mouth, the heat biting through my tongue.

'It's great.' I glanced across at my bag. 'I need to sort my clothes into the wardrobe, and there's a bookcase for my books.'

My father peered at his phone as he spoke. 'Did you bring that Richard Dawkins book I gave you for your birthday?'

I grabbed a slice of bread and tore it in half. 'I forgot. I've got the *His Dark Materials* trilogy and some Tolkien.'

He frowned at me. 'Haven't you read those before?'

The soup slipped down my throat before I could spit it at him. 'Some things are worth reading more than once.'

My father shook his head and returned his attention to the phone. My mother didn't tell him off, so I assumed it was something to do with his work. But, even after all these years of travelling the world because of his job, I still wasn't sure what he actually did. I knew it concerned the environment and green energy, which was good for the planet. So, as the wind and rain attacked the house, I guessed he must have dragged us to this isolated island for a feasibility study regarding putting more wind turbines here.

I pushed the reasons for being on Barra from my mind and concentrated on finishing the soup, desperate to get back upstairs to those photos. Tomorrow, when my parents would be too busy for me, I'd search the rest of the cottage and explore everywhere outside. My initial reluctance to come to Barra had vanished, and now that warm feeling possessing me wasn't only from the food.

* * *

The weather quickly dashed my excitement the next day. Constant rain, with thunderstorms thrown into the mix, curtailed my plans to explore outside. My father and mother retreated into their own worlds, him to work and her to write, so I spent hours going through those photos: the image where she carried a large suitcase for no apparent reason; another where she stood on the beach while the waves crashed around her ankles; the sun setting against the mist as her back was half-turned towards the camera; sitting on the rocks wearing a white hat and the strangest of long green dresses; hiding her face behind a tattered copy of *The Bell Jar*; leaning down to look at something only she could see; a pair of thick black glasses perched on the end of her nose; walking along one of the island's deserted roads; pushing a bicycle up a treacherous looking path – those and many others.

I continued to wonder what was on the CD under my pillow and got creative with the photos. They didn't appear in chronological order and couldn't be sorted by what the weather was like in them or by any physical changes in Julia's appearance. So I organised them using my system: indoor compared to outside, on land or near the sea; even smiling and not smiling. Then I laid them out like frames in a movie and created stories for them in my head, starting with the dozen taken inside my bedroom.

In her bedroom. Our bedroom.

I imagined her liking the same things I did, even though it was impossible to tell from the photos when the unknown photographer had taken them. They could have been shot at any point in the last seventy years, with no clues to their age in the clothes she wore or her hairstyle.

So, I gazed through the images in the house and created stories of her enjoying a quiet life, having come to the island to escape the noise of the modern world. Perhaps she was famous outside Barra, a YouTube star or an Instagram influencer — I knew nothing of those things, so it was possible. That idea led me to focus on the photos taken around the island, dreaming of Julia and her mysterious friend using the pictures on her social media sites. But, thinking of that annoyed me even more since I couldn't get an internet connection to use an image search to discover who Julia really was.

And maybe find out where she was now.

Could she still be on the island?

That hope kept me going during my forced exile inside the cottage, but even when creating stories for Julia in my head, the isolation and the loneliness engulfed me. With no internet and the TV only having three channels, all of which appeared to broadcast shows made fifty years before I was born, my daydreaming could only keep my brain occupied for so long. My parents kept to themselves, and we only spent time together when eating.

I continued returning to the disc, turning it over in my hands, running my fingers over its shiny surface, and fantasising about what was on it. I'd decided to risk my father's anger and use his computer to check the disk, but it wasn't possible to get to it while he was in the house. So I used our first full day on the island to copy all the photos on my phone. Now, I'd have them with me wherever I went.

I spent the rest of the time creating stories for those pictures, drifting in and out of dreams before finally falling asleep.

* * *

Day three got off to a pleasant surprise as the rain had vanished, and only a gentle wind greeted me when I poked my head outside the bedroom window. After a quick shower and a clean set of clothes, I rushed downstairs for breakfast. My father was already beavering away in the room he'd turned into a makeshift office as my mother placed a plate of beans and toast on the table in front of me.

'I'm going to Castlebay for supplies. Do you want to come?'

The beans slid down my throat before I spoke. 'Castlebay?'

She shook her head. 'You never did your homework about Barra, did you?' I didn't reply and crunched on a piece of toast. 'It's the largest village on the island, with two hotels, several guest houses and B&Bs, a range of shops, a bank, a petrol station and a hospital.'

I picked a rogue bean from between my teeth. 'Wow. I can't wait.'

She poured herself a cup of coffee, knowing I hated the smell, and frowned at me.

'Perhaps you'd rather visit the deserted village on your own.'

I used the fork to cover the toast with beans. 'What deserted village?'

My mother sipped on her drink. 'Why should I tell you

if you couldn't be bothered to do your research before we came here?'

I got my knife and squashed all the beans until the plate was swimming in an orange sauce, staring at her and recognising it hadn't taken her long to punish me for things I hadn't done. But, after three days at our new location, things were unchanged in the family dynamic. My father ignored me or criticised me for not being grown up enough, while my mother used sly words and little digs to highlight her disapproval of everything I did.

And they wondered why I was always daydreaming or escaping into fictional worlds.

I finished my breakfast. 'Fine. I'll find it myself.'

My mother dropped three sugars into her coffee. 'Balnabodach is a small township near here, overlooking Loch Obe. Down by the shore of the loch are the remains of two earlier settlements. I think there might still be an archaeological dig going on there.'

I got up and grabbed my coat from the chair. 'Great. I'll tell you all about it when I get back.'

The wind caressed my cheeks when I stepped outside, not expecting my mother to warn me to be careful. Now I was out of the house, and she'd concentrate on her shopping trip. I zipped up my jacket and headed in the opposite direction we'd come from the airport, stepping off the path and onto the land. The first thing to hit me was the lack of noise: there was no traffic din, no sounds of people talking or shouting, and no vibrations of metal machines rushing everywhere. Then I noticed the smell and aromas of the countryside and the nearby sea. I took a deep breath, for once not smelling exhaust fumes, chemicals, or street food cooking on every corner. I'd visited the countryside before, but had experienced nothing like this. All the negative feelings about coming to the island vanished after discovering the photos of Julia and sharing this force of nature.

It didn't take long to spot a series of ruins on the eastern side of the road, down the hill and approaching a body of water I assumed was Loch Obe. I scrambled through the marshy ground covered with sea-pink flowers to the stones. The loch was connected to the sea, and I saw several sheep along its edge but no people.

I removed my phone and took photos of the area. Then I flicked through the ones of Julia, searching to see if any of them were in this place. One or two of them seemed they might be, but I wasn't sure. I needed to get a better look inside the ruins. Most were only stony humps, apart from one with thick stone filled with earth, rounded corners and a single door on the side. I ran my fingers over the rock, noticing the broken fingernail I'd forgotten about, and felt the centuries against my flesh.

'They had no mod cons here.'

The woman's voice made me jump, my legs trembling as I stepped into a hole in the ground and hurt my ankle.

'Fuck,' I said.

'I'm sorry,' the woman said. 'I didn't mean to scare you.' I saw a raven sitting on the wall behind her as she came towards me. 'Are you okay?'

I ignored the pain rushing through my leg and forced a grin onto my face.

'I'm fine. Are you an islander?'

I imagined her as a Valkyrie come to catch Odin's bird, even though she looked like a librarian with those thick glasses and 1940s hairstyle.

She laughed as she spoke. 'Well, I've been here long enough to think of myself as one, but no, I'm not.' She held out a hand to me. 'I'm Sally Carlisle, the last archaeologist working on this site.'

Her skin was cold to the touch as I shook her hand.

'It must be fascinating, discovering how our ancestors lived before technology changed everything.'

Her laughter disappeared. 'It is, but it's also heart-breaking.'

I moved my foot a little to make sure I could walk on it. 'How so?'

Carlisle reached out and touched the wall at our side. 'The overall impression here is of poverty. The excavation of this house gave us a partial insight into the lifestyle of the people who settled here. The family lived directly on the earth floor with a hearth towards one end. They probably slept around this fire and cooked their meals on it. They were likely crofters, working the land they rented from the landowner.' She took a deep breath. 'Until they and the other inhabitants were forced from here.'

'What do you mean?'

Sally Carlisle pointed at me, and I half thought the raven would fly to her.

'You're not from Barra either, are you?'

I nodded. 'I came with my parents three days ago. My father has work to do here.'

She narrowed her eyes at me. 'Is he an archaeologist?'

'No, I think he's doing something with a new wind farm coming here.'

'Well,' she said. 'We certainly have the weather for it.'

'Why were people forced from the island?' I said. 'And when was this?'

'In 1850, Barra and the other islands of the Outer Hebrides were in the midst of the potato famines. The results on an over-populated island were catastrophic. Food was in short supply, and some died of starvation. Because of this, the then landlord of Barra - Colonel Gordon of Cluny - decided the only way to relieve himself of the problem was to clear a part of the population forcibly. Balnabodach was selected as one township for clearance. Four hundred and fifty islanders were forced onto ships and sent to Canada with a promise of work that never materialised.'

'That sounds terrible.'

She nodded. 'It was. People were hunted down by dogs, bound and thrown onto ships like cattle, transported overseas and abandoned in rags on the quayside. This was the fate of hundreds of men, women, and children. One young woman was said to have been seized as she was milking the family cow in the fields by the loch. She was put on a boat with nothing but the clothes she was wearing.'

'Sent somewhere she didn't want to go.'

Carlisle continued. 'The Barra contingent was nearly one-third of the estimated seventeen hundred people cleared from the colonel's lands in the Western Isles that year. It's unknown how many survived the winter. Still, Gordon, who also had estates in Aberdeenshire, flourished with his fortune boosted earlier by compensation from the British Government of £25,000 for the six plantations he owned in Tobago, which had more than a thousand enslaved people.'

I glanced at the ruins surrounding us, trying to imagine what it must have been like for those islanders forced from their homes. Invisible fingers crept into my stomach and clawed at my guts.

'And this was all legal?'

Sally Carlisle moved away from the stones as the sky darkened above.

'Unfortunately, it was.' She glanced up as drops of rain

fell. 'I think a storm is on its way.' She peered at me. 'Will you return later to explore some more?'

A cold wind bit at my face as I nodded. 'If we ever get some decent weather.' I still wanted to find the spots in Julia's photos. Then I removed my phone and showed Carlisle the images. 'Do you recognise this young woman? Her name is Julia.'

Carlisle cleaned her glasses and flicked through the pictures.

'No. Is she a relative of yours?'

As I replied, the rain got heavier, and we moved away from the ruins.

'Yeah, she's a second cousin.'

'And you don't know where she is?' I nodded. 'Perhaps you should go to the police.'

Was that a good idea? Probably not, since I'd never seen Julia outside of the photos.

'Maybe I will,' I said as we headed towards a parked car I'd somehow missed on the way to the ruins.

'Do you want a lift?'

I shook my head. 'No thanks. Our cottage is only a few minutes away.'

She got into the car and drove off. I glanced back at the deserted village and thought of all those people forcibly kicked off this place nearly two hundred years ago.

And I was still no closer to discovering who Julia was.

* * *

On our fourth day on the island, over breakfast, my father got up from the table and said he'd be away for a couple of days with work. Then he left without saying another word. My mother was indifferent to the news, but I watched him as he went, noting what he carried and barely able to contain my joy when I saw he didn't have the laptop with him.

It was late in the morning before I entered his room, restraining myself in case he returned. I thought he must have taken it as I couldn't find it anywhere, slumping to the floor in despair with the realisation I might never discover what was on the disc. My head was flat against the carpet, a knot in my stomach, when I glimpsed a dark case hiding beneath the bed.

Refusing to get my hopes up, I dragged myself across the floor, digging nails into the dusty rug like a mountain climber pulling myself up Everest. And then, just as I was about to reach for the case, the floorboards creaked outside the room. I crunched my body into the smallest shape possible and rolled under the bed on top of the thing I'd come looking for. Its corners were sticking into my stomach, but at least I knew I had what I wanted. Not that it would do me any good when he discovered me.

I clenched my teeth as the door opened, and my mother walked into the room, the Snoopy slippers she always wore instantly recognisable. Shock and relief ran through me in equal measure.

'Where have you hidden them?' she growled. It was the first time I'd heard her speak all day. She may have been upset, but she didn't tear the room apart, instead delicately checking everywhere for what she wanted, ensuring nothing looked out of place when she finished. She searched between the pages of his books, inside the cabinet, and his clothes in the wardrobe, but still couldn't find what she was looking for. Only my mother's distaste for getting down on her hands and knees stopped her from discovering me.

'I know you've put them somewhere. I'll search every spot in this house,' she said as she slammed the door behind her.

I rolled from beneath the bed. It was only as I considered how lucky I'd been that I thought of my mother finding the box of photos in my room. I scrambled up, clutched the laptop to my chest, burst out of the door and dashed to my room.

As I fell into the bedroom, I was relieved to find it empty. I crashed onto the bed and listened for the sound of my mother's footsteps. Only when I heard the front door closing and her feet crunching against the driveway did I remember I still had the laptop. I dropped it on the bed and moved to the window, pushing the curtains aside to see her heading towards the buildings nearby that stored disused machinery.

I returned to the bed, picked up the case, and turned the machine on. It was an old device, taking an age to start, so I checked if it had a mouse. I hated using the keypad on a laptop.

As I searched unsuccessfully for the device, I discovered paper pushed deep inside the case's pockets. I pulled them out, my curiosity making me forget about the mysteries of the computer disc. The screen was alive behind me as I unfolded the first piece of paper. It didn't take long to realise this was what my mother had hunted for.

I can't wait to see you again, to wrap my lips around yours and to spend all day in bed together as we did in Munich.

We'd spent six months in Germany before coming to Barra, and none of it had been in Munich. I read more before becoming embarrassed by the intimate things this unknown person had written to my father. Unlike my affection for Julia, I didn't perceive it to be love. That thought snapped me back to reality, the laptop, and why I'd taken it. I grabbed the disc from the box and slipped it into the computer. As it whirled around, I glanced at the letters, wondering about the father I'd never really known.

Was this why he was so distant from me?

Then the disc ground to a halt, and the icon appeared on the desktop. I clicked it in anticipation, my eyes widening at a collection of video files, four in all. I stared at the bright blue icons before sorting them in date order. There was a week's difference between each file, one clip filmed at the start of each week, covering a month in total. They'd been recorded precisely a year ago.

After waiting to see what was on the disc, I was surprised at how reluctant I was to watch them. What if Julia wasn't the beautiful, caring person I'd created in my imagination? I sank back into the pillows and stared at the computer screen, my eyes flicking between each video file and trying to guess what was on them based only on the date they'd been recorded. Finally, after fifteen minutes of anguished deliberation, imagining all the worst-case scenarios, I leaned over and clicked on the first one.

The clip flickered alive, and I adjusted it so it filled the screen. It looked like I was peering into a mirror as I saw my room. The bed even had the same cover. Nothing happened for thirty seconds, and my heart sank as I thought it would just be an empty video and all the others would be the same. And then the girl I'd come to love sat down on the bed and stared into the camera.

'It's soooooo boring here. And the weather is terrible.' My chest beat even faster at the sight of that pout and the sound of her irritated voice. 'There's nothing in the house, and the internet doesn't work.' Julia's eyes had widened with annoyance, those delicate lips wobbling slightly. 'It's rained non-stop for a week. It's so wet outside I feel like Noah without the menagerie.' Julia allowed herself to laugh with a smile wide enough to send tiny darts of obsession into my heart. 'I need to get out and explore. If it doesn't improve by tomorrow, I'll trudge across the mud and search through the derelict buildings next door.'

The video finished. I played it again, focusing on her voice and the sparkle in her eyes. I wanted to wait before playing the next clip, dragging out the anticipation. I hit the play button and waited for the screen to come alive.

'It's been a hectic week. Not that I've visited anywhere on the island because I've been too busy going through this.' Julia was in the bedroom again, sitting on the bed, but she had the box in front of her this time. The same one I'd discovered. 'I found this in the building next to our house, hiding away behind a broken-down car; it's my box of delights.' She picked it up and emptied all of its contents over the bed, exactly as I'd done, with photos drifting down like confetti at a wedding.

I was confused: what pictures were these?

'I've spent a week going through these images, staring at this beautiful person.' And then Julia held one of them to the computer, and I saw a brown-eyed young woman with the most beguiling smile and stunning afro hair. 'This is Anna. These are all Anna.' Julia scooped up a handful of the images and threw them into the air. They tumbled to the floor, and she stared at them with wonder in her eyes.

'I have all these photos of this gorgeous woman, but she is a mystery to me, so I'm going to scour the island to find who she is – and where she is. Look at these wonderful pictures.' And just as I'd done with the ones of Julia, she did the same with those images of Anna, laying them in rows.

'This is my favourite, the one I hold close to my heart every night.' She held the picture up to the screen, and Anna looked dazzling in a figure-hugging yellow dress painted on her hips, open seductively at her breasts, with a strap hanging wantonly from her shoulder. Her smile lit up the camera, and I could see why Julia was smitten with her. I told myself I wasn't bothered that the woman I loved appeared to be in love with someone else, but I knew I'd seen that dress before. So I stopped the video and got my box of photos.

It took me a few minutes, but I found it at the bottom of the pile. It was obvious it was the same dress where the strap hung off her shoulder. It had the same slight tear and frayed edges. As with Anna, the material stuck to Julia's body, so no contour or curve was hidden. In the photo, Julia was outside, somewhere near the ruins I visited yesterday, her legs pulled up to her chest, the dress inching its way above her knees, her hands resting on those knees, with a beaming smile brighter than the sun. I grabbed the picture and placed it next to the one still frozen on the computer – the two women were wearing the same dress. I studied the screen and contemplated what it meant. I'd fallen in love with her through a group of photographs, yet she was in love with someone else in the same manner. And they'd both worn the same dress.

I imagined what it would be like to wear that dress as I started the video again while still holding that photo.

'I must find my beautiful Anna, and I will scour this island until I do.' And then the clip finished.

I peered at the photograph before switching my gaze to the computer screen. The only way to solve the mystery was to watch the other videos.

When the third started, Julia wore faded jeans and a

cut-off pink shirt, sitting on the bed. Her legs were pulled up against her ribs like in the yellow dress photo, with a selection of pictures in front of her. She grabbed one and held it to the camera.

'I sorted through the photos, selected all the ones where Anna is outside, and went to those locations. I spoke to everyone I could, but they all denied any knowledge of her. I didn't believe a word of it. They were all hiding something. I could tell from how they turned their face from mine when I asked about her. They dropped their eyes and lowered their voices when they talked as if she'd never existed. But I discovered these.' She held up two thin-looking pieces of paper. 'The first one I found under a rock in the abandoned village at Balnabodach. And this is what it says.'

'*I have nobody here, suffering in isolation on this island. It's like a living death. The weather fluctuates between grim and terrible, but I've grown accustomed to the bleakness. I wish I had somebody to talk to.*'

She stopped speaking and folded the paper back together.

'I've read it many times, the sadness jumping from the page and into me. The second one I found is longer and more upbeat.' Julia placed it face down on the bed, reading from it with more pep in her voice.

'*I admire the island for what it is, uncompromising and forthright; it will switch between harshness and invigorating in an instant. It has taught me many important lessons about life in such a short time and about my life in particular: there can be no pleasure without pain, no beauty without ugliness. I came here to find meaning in my life, and now I think I know what it is.*'

Julia finished reading and put the paper into her trouser pocket.

'I need to discover what happened to her. I'll take some of these photos and the paper with me tomorrow to the deserted village. A woman works there, an archaeologist, who could know something about Anna.'

Was she talking about Sally Carlisle?

I played the clip again, seeing if there was anything helpful I might have missed. There was a fierce determination in her voice and behind her eyes. The video ended, and I lay back on the bed. My mother still hadn't returned, and I wondered if she'd given up what she was searching for.

There was an unexpected urge to speak to my mother, to seek advice regarding the many emotions I was feeling. I got up to look out the window, but there was no sign of her. Instead, I stared at the last video on the laptop. There was a sliver of fear in my heart about what the final clip would reveal – would Julia have answered the mystery of Anna, and would that help me discover the whereabouts of Julia? I hit the play button again.

'I understand why Anna kept returning to this point.' She held several photos of Anna with a derelict building in the background, a place I recognised: the ruin of the house I'd stood outside yesterday. 'I felt the same emotional awakening she must have at that spot; a beginning and ending that will complete us both. I know now where to find her, where I must go. And what I must do.'

Then the video ended. As I closed the laptop screen, I heard my mother returning, slamming the door behind her. I pushed the box of photos under the bed, picked up my father's letters, and ran downstairs, thrusting the papers into her hands.

'This is what you were looking for.'

My mother's stony expression changed, her mouth open wide enough to swallow a plate. I left her grasping at the letters and went outside, greeted by a cloudless sky. For once, neither wind nor rain harassed me as I dashed to the deserted village.

But I had one constant companion.

A raven flew with me, only a few feet above my head. I ignored it, focusing on the treacherous marshy ground as I headed for the spot where I'd seen Sally Carlisle. Julia had visited those stones, stood within the remains of that house, and I had to see inside the derelict building. Perhaps there would be something to strengthen the connection I had with her.

The bird reached the ruins first. I clutched at my chest, taking a deep breath as the mist from the loch drifted over the land. It took a minute for my heart to settle, my head clearing as the haze increased and visibility became near impossible. The loch's surface disappeared, as did the sky, and all I could see was the closest ruin and the raven waiting for me.

I trudged towards it before stopping a few feet away. I removed my mobile phone and found the photos of Julia at the derelict house. When I looked up again, the bird had vanished. The remains of the stone walls only reached my hips as I stepped inside them, but it immediately felt as if centuries of history surrounded me. I remembered what Sally Carlisle had told me about the families struggling to live on this island before being forced off it and transported to Canada.

The mist crept into the ruins like a ghost, glistening around me. The raven beat its wings somewhere beyond my vision, and I knew there was nothing here to help me find

Julia. So I pressed my way through the haze and stumbled outside.

The wind returned and pushed the wispy vapour out of my eyes, my heart sinking with the realisation I'd have to get my mother to take me to Castlebay so I could question the locals about Julia. And that would mean she'd find out about the photos and videos, leading to more of her ridicule.

I was about to put my phone away when I heard the dogs barking.

That was followed by shouts and screams ahead of me. The air cleared, but I couldn't see who was making the noise. Urgency sped through me as I ran towards the commotion, hearing strong Scottish accents that made it impossible to understand what they were saying.

Before moving any closer, somebody grabbed me and pulled me into the bushes.

'Dinnae let thaim see ye, or ye'll end up oan th' ship wi' th' ithers.'

The accent was broad, but I understood her. She let go of my arm, and I stared into pale blue eyes. The girl looked younger than me, dressed in clothes that were barely rags and with dark rings under her eyes.

'What's happening?' I said.

She gazed at me as if seeing me for the first time.

'Whit urr ye sportin'?'

I didn't understand her words. 'Sportin'?'

She pointed at my trousers. 'Girls dinnae wear breeks. Urr ye yin o' Gordon's agents?'

Gordon's agents? Her words triggered a memory of something Sally Carlisle had told me.

'What year is this?'

She looked at me as if I was insane.

And maybe I was.

'1850.'

I grabbed the nearest bush, the thorns digging into my hand and drawing blood. I watched it drip from my fingers and onto the grass. The barking grew closer as I spoke.

'Have you seen any other girls dressed like me?'

Is this what happened to Julia and Anna? Were they transported in time as I appeared to have impossibly done?

She narrowed her dark eyes at me. 'Whaur urr ye fae?'

'Where am I from? You wouldn't believe me if I told you.'

She shook her head. 'It disnae maiter. We hae tae git awa' fae Gordon's agents.'

But where could I go now I was stuck in the past?

A thick smell of smoke drifted over us, irritating my lungs, so I bent over and coughed into the grass.

'Gordon's agents ur pure burnin' th' houses,' the girl said.

I cleared my throat and got up, peering at where the loch met the sea. Small boats were ferrying people to a larger ship.

Then I saw the men with their dogs, forcing islanders towards more waiting boats. Confusion and noise reigned. The hounds barked and yapped while people could only sob and scream. I heard mothers and children asking fathers and husbands where they were going. Big, strong men were pushed forward like cattle and beaten down if they dared protest.

I turned to the girl. 'Where can we go?'

Darkness covered her face. 'A dinnae ken.'

My legs trembled as I moved from the safety of the bushes, searching for the ruins that had transported me here. Only they wouldn't be ruins, but a complete house in this time.

But there was nothing but the countryside and the sea.

And the ship with its reluctant passengers waiting to journey to Canada.

That's when I knew there was only one place to go if I was to find Julia.

*   *   *

As Clara raced towards the ship, the photographs in her room changed, and she got her wish to wear that yellow dress.

The Last Rites of Oscar Wilde

My oldest enemy had invited me to his home. It was the third invite in as many weeks. I considered dumping it in the bin with the others, but this one was different.

Come if you want to watch the only moving images of Oscar Wilde.

I put the card next to the autographed photo of Louise Brooks in *American Venus* and scrutinised the scrawl of William Lincoln. I hadn't seen or spoken to Buffalo Bill in twenty years, and now he claimed to have a film of Oscar Wilde. It was preposterous. He'd waited two decades for his revenge, and this was the best he could do.

I considered Lincoln's text as a scratched version of Robert Johnson's *Cross Road Blues* span on the turntable. He'd gained the nickname Buffalo Bill thirty years ago as a trader of unique artistic goods. His fondness for wearing a Wild West American hat and his extravagant goatee beard was the name's supposed source, but I knew it was more to do with his unethical methods of acquiring his stock. This unscrupulous behaviour made it easy for me to sell him a fake Abbott and Costello movie. When he unveiled it to the public as genuine, it didn't take long before his reputation fell apart. This was cemented when I anonymously leaked how *Abbott and Costello Meet the Robots* was created using new digital technology and clips of dead actors. The film cost a lot of money but was worth it to ruin my only competitor for rare popular culture items.

His mansion was gone, and now he lived in some dingy flat on the other side of the city. I smiled at how such an arrogant man had fallen so low because of his greed. I picked up Lincoln's card again. What harm would it do to visit him? There was no Wilde film, but what if he had other things, items he'd kept all this time after his disgrace? It had been a while since I'd purchased anything with the WOW factor, so perhaps it would be worth it.

The bourbon kissed the back of my throat as I phoned the number on the card. It rang twice before he picked up. 'Peter, how good to hear from you.'

I wasn't in the mood for small talk. 'There's no such thing as moving images of Oscar Wilde, William.' I refused to call him Buffalo Bill. 'Even you can't get away with such a lie.'

'Well, Peter, you did with Bud and Lou, didn't you?' I was right; this was about what I'd done to him twenty years ago. 'But that's all water under the bridge. This is genuine; three minutes of a silent film of Wilde playing his most famous creation.'

'Dorian Gray?'

'The same.' His breath rasped down the line. 'And I have to be honest, Peter; my health isn't the best. I have to pass this on to someone who understands the significance of it. This is my legacy.'

So, the rumours were true about his illness. 'A film featuring Oscar Wilde would be priceless, William.'

'I don't care about money, Peter.' The words wheezed out of him. 'Will you come and see it?'

What had I to lose? Even if it was a perfect fake, I could advertise it like that and still recoup on it. 'Is seven o'clock tomorrow night okay?'

'I'll dig out my finest bottle of bourbon.'

We said our farewells, and I ended the call. Then, as I considered what the entertainment value would be, I slipped the needle back onto the record and listened to Robert Johnson's voice speak to me from the past.

* * *

Lincoln's flat was as horrible as I'd expected: the paint peeled from the damp walls, old newspapers and magazines were strewn over the floor, and it stank of cats. He looked little better, having grown a face-covering grey beard since I'd seen him last and gone utterly bald on top. The lines under his eyes were so many and thick they could have transported trains across them. He handed me a bourbon as I sat down.

'It's good to see you, old friend.' Maybe his mind had departed, considering we'd never been friends. Or perhaps he'd forgotten what I'd done to him. His next words ended that thought. '*Abbott and Costello Meet the Robots* still makes me smile.'

I sipped at the drink, wondering if he'd brought me here to poison me. 'You enjoyed it, then?'

'Peter, I don't hate the film for being a forgery.'

'But you can hate me?'

He raised his glass in my direction. 'At first, I did.' The glint in his eye reflected off the glass. 'And possibly for a

105

decade after, but you can't hold a grudge forever, can you? Plus, you sold it to me expertly.'

I bit through a sizeable chunk of ice. 'Abbott and Costello had met Dracula, Frankenstein, the Mummy, the Killer, the Invisible Man, Captain Kidd and other strange villains in their movies, so why not robots? Throwing in the Asimov connection was a nice touch, I thought.'

'No, that was getting Lugosi to play the mad scientist with the robot army and having Frances Farmer as his assistant.' He finished his drink and poured himself another one. 'The technology used to recreate the actors amazed me; so good it convinced me of its authenticity.'

His nostalgia bored me. 'Is that why you told me the tale of a fake Oscar Wilde movie? Do you want revenge?'

Lincoln put his glass on the dusty table next to him. 'No, Peter; I lost my anger an age ago. I spent my free time in more positive avenues and found a new hobby. And that's how I discovered the copy of *The Picture of Dorian Gray*.' He reached into his pocket and removed a remote control. He used it to turn on the gigantic screen to my right. 'It was filmed in France around 1897 or '98, after Wilde's release from prison. It's rumoured to have been shot at the Lumière brothers' Paris studio.'

I smiled at him. 'The more fantastical lie, the easier it is to tell. You should have been a politician, William.'

'Why don't you watch it and see for yourself, old friend.' He reached up and turned off the lights, and the familiar sound of a projector cut through the silence. I drank some more bourbon and gazed at the screen.

The opening scene was of a room full of furniture as the camera crept towards a painting on the wall, covered by an enormous piece of cloth. Then a man entered the frame, striding for the canvas before turning to the lens. I leant closer as the actor did the same: he was the spitting image of Wilde from the photographs of him in the late nineteenth century. He opened his lips, but nothing came out; of course not, this was silent. He was agitated, with puffed-out cheeks and eyes bulging as he shouted at the camera. This lasted a minute before he returned to the painting. He hesitated at first, seemingly unsure of what was behind it. I knew what it was, expecting a poor imitation of horror when he whipped away the cover, but I grabbed at my face when he did.

'It's shocking for the time, isn't it?'

Hell ravaged Gray's face with disfigured features. One puss-filled eye slipped below the nose, while the other, black as the night, pointed towards the forehead. The mouth twisted out of shape, with maggots bursting from the lips; the skin mottled and scarred, full of boils and pock-marks. As I bit against my hand, the film flickered to the end, rattling somewhere behind me. I finished the drink and calmed my nerves.

'It's good, William, I'll give you that, but it's still a fake.'

He grinned at me. 'It's as real as you or I, Peter; why would I lie to you?'

'For revenge.'

'After twenty years.' He laughed. 'I'm not that patient.'

'So, where did you acquire it? What's its provenance?'

'I have sources in France, where it's lain since completion, locked away for over a century.'

I'd had enough of his nonsense and went to stand, but my legs wouldn't move. How foolish I'd been. 'You drugged me.'

He shook his head. 'No, Peter; the film has you now.'

My vision spun, and he drifted in and out of focus as my mouth dried up, and I struggled to breathe.

'What..., what..., do you mean?'

'After his release from imprisonment, Wilde pursued revenge on the man he blamed for putting him behind bars: John Douglas, the 9th Marquess of Queensberry. When he arrived in France, he sought many shamans and mystics, and they helped him with the movie.'

'Mysticism?' I wanted to laugh in his face, but I could hardly move my lips.

'Wilde filmed this clip on film stock inscribed with certain runic symbols. The mystics then connected it to another item with the last symbol to finish the spell. Whoever holds this object and watches the movie is caught in the trap.'

'What object?'

He nodded towards my hand. 'The glass you hold.' He got up, took it from me and pointed at the symbol on the bottom.

I was about to speak when I blacked out.

* * *

When I woke, I was somewhere else, inside a black and white room with a covered painting on the wall. Something compelled me to pull it off, but I turned behind me instead and shouted at the space where the camera should have been.

If only I'd known.

Hellgrazer

Demons have a terrible reputation, which is understandable considering the horrible things we've done, but that's only because humans are unaware of the good we do as well.

My name is Zero Chance; my parents had a peculiar sense of humour. When I was ten, my father told me they'd given me that moniker to inspire me to do something significant with my life, something inspirational for others. So I ended up as the accountant of the biggest criminal organisation in the country. If my mother and father had known, they would have found that knowledge, and me, loathsome. But their freak encounter with a plummeting piece of glass saved them from such disappointment.

'Think about your future,' my father told me on my thirteenth birthday.

So I did. And after considerable research, there was no denying that organised crime would always be profitable, regardless of time or location. Every person who steps beyond the law has a good reason for doing it, and I was no different. The problem was I had too much ambition and not enough connections. I could spend forty years working for someone else as they lived the good life – as my old man had done – while feeling content because I had a decent house, car, and wife.

However, I wanted more than decent. I desired what the one per cent had.

And crime was the only way for me to get it.

My employers provided me with two rooms in an office in a converted factory by the river, plus Veronica, my secretary. I convinced myself that running the money through several bank accounts didn't mean I held any responsibility for the murder, robbery, extortion, intimidation, drug dealing, or human trafficking, which caused the cash flow.

For ten years, everything ran smoothly. I took the money, washed it clean, and then siphoned it back to them minus a small cut for myself. I never had to see a dead body or hear the cries of the oppressed. Nevertheless, I thought it might play on my mind, especially when some terrible brutal crime was on the news. Yet it didn't.

Of course, it couldn't last.

Veronica presented me with the pact that changed everything. She'd come with the place when I got the job, waiting for me patiently the first afternoon I'd staggered in, recovering from another hangover. Teetering at nearly six feet tall in those five-inch heels, her amber eyes peered into mine as she waited for me to deliver the first command of Chance Accountants. Ten years later, those eyes burnt fiercely within a face sculpted from a black and white Hollywood movie star, with cascading golden tresses that bewitched and charmed all who fell into her orbit. It hadn't taken me long to realise my new employers had placed her there to observe and seduce me rather than for any secretarial skills.

But I hadn't complained.

That was then. Now, something far more wanton and dangerous possessed her. My crimes against humanity had awoken a creature from below, and it had come calling to make me an offer I couldn't refuse.

'I have two propositions for you, Mr Chance.' She sat in my chair, her pencil-thin skirt clinging to her curves like liquid glue. The voice was still hers, but I also knew it wasn't. Something wicked had come this way. She had an old-looking pamphlet under her arm, which she placed on my desk amongst financial and legal documents.

'*The Tragical History of the Life and Death of Doctor Faustus.*'

I said the words aloud, hoping they might break the spell I was drowning in.

'It's dated now, but I like to bring it with me, so the more intelligent of my prospective clients will recognise what was happening without me having to, shall we say, expose my true self.' The grin was so sharp it could have sliced flesh straight from the bone and probably had on many occasions. I sank into the chair usually reserved for hired thugs and waited for my fate to reveal itself. 'You can come and work for me or....'

'Or what?'

Her smile melted my heart. 'You'll become something new, Mr Chance. You'll be shit on the bottom of someone else's shoe, the bedraggled thing that perennially crawls out of the sewer to nuzzle up to dogs, the turd that won't flush, the dirt that won't wash off the windows. You'll be what's left in Jeffrey Dahmer's fridge and the ground that pigs die on.'

It wasn't a hard sell. So I went for the first option and signed the contract.

I was only one of the minor minions gathering up

insignificant souls whose time had nearly elapsed. As a result, I didn't get to meet influential people, royalty or celebrities; those were for demons with far more experience than me.

But then that changed. For reasons still unknown to me, I was standing at the front of the biggest concert of the year, staring at the most famous band in the world. And all because I was there to collect the greatest rock star on the planet.

The venue was nearly as hot as where I'd come from, with thousands of sweating bodies cramped together and pushed violently against the walls. Yet, none of it affected me as I stared into the face of Bobby Ace and considered how to remove him from his place of worship and into his eternal realm of suffering.

Some souls we gather for punishment are well deserving of what they're about to receive, and for him, it was long overdue. Twenty years ago, his parents and younger sister were tortured and murdered. Thankfully, the legend goes, young Bobby was on a camping trip with three mates at the time and was lucky to escape the horrible fate that befell the rest of his family. But, like all legends, most of that tale was fabricated.

He was with friends that night but not on vacation; they watched while he killed those he hated: parents who loved him and a sister he was jealous of. The Boss was also there, slipping the document Bobby had gleefully signed into the inside pocket of her fashionable Armani jacket. So Bobby Ace became the rock superstar he'd always dreamed of, and his mates played the instruments behind him.

Their time would come later; they were not my responsibility. But he certainly was, and it was a big gig for me, so I had to choose the appropriate removal method. I could rise to the stage, unnoticed by everybody in the arena but the band, and slowly squeeze the life from his corrupt heart and give him a classic rock star death. Or I could wait until he was on the toilet, trousers sprawled around his ankles, delivering something much more inglorious.

I decided the second option would be worthier of the tawdry piece of human flesh gyrating his riddled narcotic body towards the teenage girls leering below him. So I moved between them and stared deep into his eyes, my gaze descending until it got an anchor on his soul. He felt my presence well before his face found mine, and I revealed my true self to him.

As the rest of the band played, he paused when he should have sung torturous lyrics about death and warriors transported to Valhalla. It would have been an appropriate time to take him then, a mythical end for him, but I was already set on providing him with the eternal shame he so richly deserved. I could make him weep and shit himself on stage, a sight that would last for eternity. Instead, I smiled as he tried to regain his composure.

Then he threw his guitar across the stage and held his arms above his head. Slowly, the others stopped playing, and expectations rose throughout the arena. Even I was curious about what he was doing.

'My friends, I have something important to tell you.' His voice wavered, still out of breath from his warbling and the shock of seeing me. A hush descended everywhere, strobe lights flickering above our heads. 'I have a confession to make.' I ignored him for a second and looked at the rest of the band; they were as surprised as everybody else.

'This won't save you, Robert.' Only he heard me.

But he continued.

'Twenty years ago, I did a horrible thing, and now is the

time for you all to hear the truth; for the world to know the truth.' He stopped peering into the faces of his spellbound followers and grinned at me instead, a look that said *I'm too clever for you and your Boss.* 'To my eternal shame, I've kept a terrible secret from all of you.' Another pause for effect. 'With the help of the band, I murdered my parents and sister, and I must confess to everything.'

The place erupted in shock; the drummer slumped to the floor while the other two stared at each other. Bobby thought he'd won; that time behind bars would spare him from eternal damnation, if even for a little while. I could have taken him then, but he knew I wouldn't while he'd left so many questions unanswered. Everything descended into chaos as he snuck off stage and into his manager's arms.

He grinned at me as he went. 'Better to be in jail than with your Boss.'

I slipped away, disappointed I'd blown it, and wondered if I'd get such an important job again.

Then I got a text on my phone.

'Well done. Mr Ace has thirty years of suffering in prison to look forward to before joining us. And he will suffer once the world discovers the true horror of his crimes. And his reputation is ruined for all eternity.'

I felt good as I strode into the cool night air as all around me, angry people threw shirts adorned with Bobby Ace's face to the ground and trampled them into the dirt.

Pauline Pope's Paranormal Detective Agency

It was a momentous day for Pauline Pope for two reasons: celebrating her sixteenth birthday and the first time a living human had offered her work.

'What exactly does a paranormal detective do?'

Pauline ignored him and reached for one of her birthday cards. It was a vibrant shade of red and stank of three-day-old eggs. As she opened it, a sinister laugh erupted from the middle, sounding like a pneumatic chain smoker spewing up the last of their lungs. It stopped after five seconds, replaced by a female voice whispering *happy sixteenth birthday to you* in a style reminiscent of Marilyn Monroe. It was inappropriate for a girl her age, but typical of her Aunt Zora. Not that she was really her aunt. Or even human.

She grabbed another envelope and peered at the man who'd asked the question. Jack Sol looked like a heavy-weight boxer, barely fitting his impressive physique into the flimsy chair Pauline thought would never be used; after all, the dead don't need to sit. As she waited for the seat to split in half, she replied to the owner of the world's biggest bank.

'I perform conflict resolution for the supernatural.'

The rich man glowered at the teenager through sceptical eyes. 'Such things exist?'

'Why else would you be here?'

Pauline opened the envelope to find it empty, wondering who was trying to wind her up this time. She shook the paper and threw it onto the desk, and a cloud of fine purple powder slithered from it. She tried not to breathe it, but it was too late. It smelt of rose petals and a pinch of ginger. Pauline pushed her fingers against her neck to cough the dust from her throat. It was to no avail. The old man and his guards did the same as she gazed at the purple flecks scattered on their cheeks.

This will be interesting.

She waited for the effects to start, but nothing happened, and she cursed her luck; delayed reaction, no telling when it would kick in. Pauline hoped it would be sooner rather than later since she hated surprises. She returned to her prospective client.

He swallowed the purple dust, his lungs protesting with dregs of phlegm flying from his mouth and hitting the wall beside her. She made a mental note to add the cleaning costs to his bill. The rich man regained his composure, the enforced colour receding from his skin, while his wide, frog-like eyes shrunk into his flabby cheeks. He called for his security in the shadows to step forward. The guard opened the laptop and played a video clip. Pauline moved closer to get a better view of the screen while Sol studied her.

'It's the private vault in our largest bank. There's ten million on the table, or at least there was.' Then, just as Pauline was coming to terms with what that amount of money looked like, the scene changed. The banknotes floated up and hovered in the air briefly before disappearing. 'This has happened four times; forty million vanished.' Sol struggled to contain his irritation. 'My people have checked every scientific possibility and got nothing. So I came to you.' He couldn't keep the desperation and scorn from his voice. 'You're fifteen, and you talk to ghosts?'

'Sixteen today, and I do more than talk.'

She whispered arcane words which only a few would understand, and she appeared: Amy, the eighteen-year-old girl who'd fallen off a bridge six months ago. She threw her arms around the paranormal detective.

'Happy birthday, Pauline!'

As Amy squeezed her, the security guards lunged forward with guns pointed at the dead teenager. Jack Sol was a vision of shock, his eyes threatening to burst from his head.

'How did you do that?'

Sweat ran down his face even though the temperature had dropped to colder than inside a fridge. Pauline ignored the question and focussed on the teenager. Treating her like this as an exhibition to show off her abilities wasn't fair.

'Do you want me to deal with these people, Pauline?' Amy glared at the security cowering before her, their faces etched with confusion at the sight of the skinny girl shimmering in and out of existence.

'No, Amy, it's fine.' She turned to Sol. 'I'll take the job, but you must let me inside the vault.'

He gazed at the giggling ghost. 'Agreed. And we leave now.'

Sol didn't wait for her to respond. He headed out of the door with his security scampering behind him.

'Can I come with you?' At least Amy was excited.

Pauline stared at her; being dead didn't make a ghost immune to danger. There were worst places than where she'd been the past six months. 'Yes, as long as you promise to behave.'

Amy grinned and pirouetted like a demented ballerina. 'Well, I'll need fresh clothes and a trip to the hairdresser.'

After Pauline had explained to Amy the rules of her new existence, she'd been aggrieved by the knowledge once you entered a spirit realm, your appearance at the point of death would never change. She ran her fingers through her giant Afro, but her bright yellow jumpsuit annoyed her.

'Keep yourself hidden unless I say otherwise. No unnecessary shocks.' They left the office and went outside. Pauline gathered her thoughts as they climbed into the limousine.

'Did you get my birthday present?' Amy pulled something small and unliving from the top of her head. She dropped it at the feet of the security sitting opposite. They shrank in fear when they realised it wasn't a mouse. It scampered past their shoes and disappeared somewhere under the front seat.

'Was that your card with the purple powder inside?' She wanted to be mad at her, but found it impossible.

Amy shook her head. 'Nope, not me. I got you Houdini's spell book for your birthday. Didn't it arrive?'

She couldn't tell her Houdini's spell book went up in flames fifty years ago. Instead, they settled into small talk regarding the latest developments on *Love Island*. Twenty minutes later, they reached the bank, ushered inside via a side door, flanked by more security.

'You'll have to wear this.' The largest of the men held two blindfolds for their visitors. 'It's Mr Sol's orders. No outsiders can see where the vault is.'

Amy laughed while Pauline raised the mask to her eyes.

'And her,' said the one with the unmoving face and head balder than an egg.

It was Pauline's turn to laugh. 'Who?' she said as Amy vanished. Six confused security guards reached for their guns and stared at the empty space. Pauline didn't have time to grin before rough fingers grabbed her and guided her forward. Two minutes later, they bundled her into an elevator, and someone removed her blindfold. She was surprised to see Amy standing there in the realm only she could observe. The tears in Amy's eyes shocked her.

'Pauline, there's so much death and suffering here.' She said nothing and waited for her to continue. 'At least a dozen people have died in the corridor, but something terrible has happened to them. They're trapped between realms, half in the next life, the rest elsewhere. Their faces contorted in agony, hands grasping for help.' Amy may have been dead, but there was more humanity in her voice than Pauline heard from most of the living. She wanted to console her but couldn't until they were away from prying eyes.

'I'll meet you on the other side,' Pauline said. She watched Amy disappear as the chief guard replied to a question he wasn't asked.

'We won't be leaving your side, girl.'

The elevator stopped, and the doors opened. She stepped into the vault and gazed at the empty table in the middle of the room, transfixed by the strand of ectoplasm floating above it. What Amy had said was impossible; what she stared at was extremely difficult.

To move things from the living world into the other realms took great power, skill, and experience. The red strands entangled with the yellow told Pauline a novice had taken the cash, but it was still impressive. It also meant it was an easy trail to track. She looked up and into the hidden cameras.

'I can find your money only if I follow the thief. I need your permission to do that and your agreement to pay my fee.'

The response was instantaneous: 'I agree to both.'

Pauline wasted no time and phased into the next realm, throwing her arms around a distraught Amy.

'Something isn't right here, Pauline. I don't trust these people.'

'I don't either, but I've got to find out who was powerful enough to do this. Whatever happened here will have to wait.'

'Shall I come with you?'

She admired Amy's bravery but couldn't take the risk of both of them jumping into the unknown. 'No, but I appreciate the offer. If you feel up to it, you can check out the rest of this place; otherwise, wait here for me.'

Pauline hugged her before returning to the vault. Then she reached in her pocket for the coin her father had given her. It would be the anchor to keep her tethered to the bank. She flipped it between her fingers, just as he'd taught her, before placing it on the table. On the coin, the head of a Roman Emperor gazed at the ceiling as Pauline grabbed the floating ectoplasm and waited for the journey to begin.

The room disappeared as the colours in the air transformed into a vibrating rainbow covering her body. She had done this many times before, but it always felt strange. There was an electric buzz clinging to her, static running down her flesh and the smell of burning copper engulfing her senses. Reds, yellows and purples flickered around her head, hurting her eyes as she gripped the coin, which cut into her palm. A high-pitched guitar sound shrieked in her skull.

The sensation lasted only a few seconds before Pauline landed at the thief's destination, her feet hitting the ground with a thud and the vibrating colours disappearing from her view. She dropped the coin into her pocket as her ears returned to normal, apart from a slight ringing.

The place was enormous and deserted. A quick glimpse around her new surroundings and Pauline saw the empty beds, the broken medical equipment and the dirty stationery stamped with St Claire's Hospital. She recognised the name and knew it had closed years ago. The emptiness was perplexing since it should have been overrun with ghosts.

As she pondered that conundrum, a voice shouted from upstairs. She followed it up; checking her pocket to ensure her tether to the vault was still there. The phantom version of the coin would stop her from having to walk the twenty miles back to the city.

The sounds got louder as she reached the top. Pauline stepped over broken test tubes and disused syringes to stand outside the door of the old geriatric ward. Inside, she saw the missing cash dumped on the floor. Beyond that was a boy no older than her. The kid stopped talking and turned his gaze towards her.

'Your reputation precedes you, Pauline Pope, but this is none of your concern.' He seemed familiar, but she couldn't place from where.

'Why steal this money? Where did you get the power to do it?' She inched her way into the room.

'I have a generous benefactor, something you'd know about.' Pauline froze. If an Unnamed was helping him, then she was in more trouble than she wanted. 'Have you not recognised me yet?'

And then she saw it; the age gap had thrown her. 'You're him, Sol, only younger.'

'Thirty years younger, the twin brother he murdered so he could steal the legacy our father left to me.'

Pauline had met many ghosts who bore long-time grudges, but this made little sense.

'Three decades of wallowing in your hatred wouldn't give you the power to do this.'

The younger Sol was keen to continue. 'Of course, all I've been able to do is watch him get richer every year and fail in my attempts at haunting him. Until I received the energy I needed.'

Pauline saw it eating away inside of him by the minute. 'That energy is destroying you. You've lost your chance to move on to your last resting place; all that awaits you is eternal pain in the Void.'

A shiver ran down her spine at the mention of the Void. But it wasn't the thought of that realm which paralysed her; that resulted from the purple haze drifting over them. Her unknown birthday present had returned to haunt her.

'Are you lost for words, Pauline?'

Sol lunged at her, and they fell to the floor, ghostly fingers squeezing Pauline's throat, translucent nails digging into her skin and drawing blood. Pain surged through her, electricity seeping into her veins and poisoning her bones. Her arms were like bricks glued to her side. She forced her knees into his chest. Deep inside her, Pauline found the energy to push him across the room, using fire dragged from another realm into the human world as a weapon. The purple haze vanished.

Ectoplasm leaked from him in bunches, spilling over the

floor like spaghetti from an upturned plate. Sol ignored his distress, consumed with a desire to harm the teenager before him. Pauline saw the air shimmering over the ghost, recognising how the supernatural light was bending reality around them. Sol's descent into the Void was seconds away. The familiar scent of burnt copper was everywhere.

'Why would an Unnamed help you?' This was about more than brotherly revenge. Sol opened his mouth to speak, clutching at the space in front of him, but his voice had gone, and the rest was soon to follow. 'Tell me what you did?' She shouted so hard the back of her throat stretched to the point of breaking.

Dust swirled around Sol's feet, creating a tornado of supernatural energy spinning up his legs and towards his chest. His face lost the last of its faded colour, turning translucent as unseen hands grabbed Sol and dragged him into the frozen blackness of the realm to end all realms.

Pauline waited until the door to the Void closed before approaching where Sol was sucked into the abyss. She stared at the cold concrete in the vague hope his last words would float through the stone and tell her why one of the Unnamed had given him some of its power. As far as she knew, the most powerful creatures in all the realms still couldn't cross over to Earth. Her heart beat quicker than it should at the thought of such a thing happening again. She placed her hand on the floor, feeling its frozen texture warm her fingers. Pauline was satisfied everything was okay for now. All that remained was to inform her client of where to find his missing money. She checked her pockets, but the coin wasn't there; she must have lost it in the fight.

'Damn!'

Without the tether, there was no quick return to the bank; unless there was a remnant left of the ectoplasm she used to get to the hospital. Pauline sprinted down the steps and raced to where she'd entered the building. There was a whiff of hot metal in the air, but she couldn't see what she needed, no sight of tethered strands. She had no choice but to text the address to her client, so he'd come and collect his stolen cash. At least the walk back would give her time to think of what to tell Jack Sol. She couldn't mention his brother without telling him about the involvement of the Unnamed. And she wasn't prepared to explain that to those who knew nothing about the other realms.

She texted the details to the number he'd given her in the office. Then she set off on the long walk to the city, wanting to escape before his men arrived. She was on the road for twenty minutes before the four black cars swept past her in the opposite direction.

Fifteen minutes later, they'd removed the last of the money from the hospital. All the security was concerned about was counting it and loading it into the van. And that was why nobody noticed the thing without a name in the corner, watching them as they left, expertly rolling the ancient Roman coin between its inhuman fingers. Its voice was deep and rasping as it spoke to an empty room.

'I have you now, Pauline Pope.'

Some Tea for the Devil

Kirby Sigston had grown indifferent to his forename. He'd hated it as a kid, having his parents name him after the village where he was born. And it got worse for him, aged seven, when they moved to the closest town so he could attend a bigger primary school. The other kids tormented him mercilessly from day one. Only two children treated him kindly, and they became his best friends for the next twenty years.

That was until they betrayed him.

Kirby's best friend was James Ivory; Serena Dane had been Kirby's girlfriend. Then he discovered they'd been cheating on him for months. That pain was terrible enough, but it got worse when they kicked him out of his group.

'We're going to be a duo,' Serena had told him as she gave Kirby the necklace he'd bought for her twenty-fifth birthday. He'd clasped the jewellery in his trembling hands while staring into her cerulean blue eyes.

'A synth band,' he'd stuttered. 'You want to be Yazoo.'

They'd played rock music together for four years, the

three of them, as The Hex Pistols. And now they'd kicked him out to be bloody Yazoo.

'It's more like a modern version of the Pet Shop Boys,' Serena had said as she ignored his gaze and stared at her phone. Kirby assumed she was already working on their social media accounts for the new band.

'We'll still be friends, right?' he'd murmured as she'd turned her back on him, walking towards the car and the waiting James Ivory. His former best friend hadn't had the decency to speak to Kirby about any of it, not even to apologise.

He'd watched them drive away, letting the summer drizzle slip into his eyes to mask the tears gathering there. His waterworks weren't caused by sadness but by the anger bubbling inside him, a human volcano transforming his blood into lava. Kirby stared at the necklace in his hand before ripping the chain apart and tossing it into the gutter at his feet.

That was the day he plotted his revenge.

He returned to his basement flat covered in music posters, with every surface containing CDs, LPs and old seven-inch singles. Kirby grabbed the scraps of paper of the lyrics to their newest songs, playing the heavy rock inside his head that had inspired him to write the latest tracks.

'The Devil has the best tunes,' he'd told Serena and James. 'We must do something controversial to get the media's attention.' They'd stared at him through astonished eyes, their mouths open wide enough to fit the gatefold sleeve of *The Dark Side of the Moon* inside.

'What do you mean?' Serena said.

Kirby rolled up his shirt and showed them his latest tattoo.

James laughed. 'A pentagram?'

Kirby grinned at them. 'Nobody talks about the Devil anymore, so that's what we'll do. We'll sing about Satan, demons, and blood sacrifices. It will get everybody talking about us. And it goes with the name, The Hex Pistols.'

They'd never liked the name, but he didn't care since it was his group. And now, it would be a solo venture.

They'd whispered to each other before turning to him. That's when they'd given him the double whammy.

'We don't want you in the band anymore, Kirby,' James said.

'And I'm leaving you to live with James,' Serena had added.

He'd stood there speechless, wondering how he'd never noticed something was going on between them. But he'd been too busy with his research, reading about Lucifer and how to summon the Devil.

Now, back in his flat with the rain dripping off him, he peered at what he'd gathered from books and online. Most of it was rubbish created by sad loners in their goth bedrooms, but he was sure there had to be something in there that would help him.

Not to write more music.

But to get revenge on them.

To summon Satan to torture and kill Serena and James.

Kirby went to the stereo and dropped the needle onto the record on the turntable. He ran his fingers through his wet hair, imagining the liquid as blood soaking the heads of those who'd betrayed him. He listened to Led Zeppelin's *Houses of the Holy* and returned to his research, trawling through web pages and documents detailing the connection between music and selling your soul to the Devil in a Faustian exchange for musical greatness.

The first example he read was something he was

already aware of, the tale of Robert Johnson, a Mississippi-born musician who supposedly sold his soul to Satan. According to the myth, the transaction transformed Johnson from an average itinerant musician into one of the greatest guitarists of all time. And the legend of the man who composed *Hell Hound on My Trail* was only strengthened by his mysterious death, possibly a murder, at twenty-seven.

The more Kirby read about musicians and Satan, the greater he believed he could summon the Prince of Darkness. So he sped through the recollections of 70s rock stars and their Devil worship – even John Lennon claimed he'd sold his soul to the Devil to guarantee the Beatles' success – devouring tales of heavy metal and Satanism, blood ritual and sacrifices, and the development of death metal.

By the time he got to the site dedicated to the infamous occult figure Aleister Crowley, Kirby was desperate to discover the secret of how to summon the Devil. He spent hours trawling through the information, sorting out the nonsense from those that might hold the key to his needs, copying dozens of supposed ways of contacting Satan. When he fell asleep in front of the computer, he'd gathered pages of material, all waiting for him when he woke from his dreams of revenge, gruesome murders, and becoming the most famous musician in the world.

And it wasn't the only thing sitting there when he opened his eyes.

'I much prefer modern dance music over that testosterone-fuelled guitar wank designed for perpetual teenage boys.'

Kirby rubbed the sleep from his face, staring at the woman sitting opposite him who was eating a candy bar and drinking tea. She wore a smart blue suit, and for a second, he thought his bank manager had visited to chastise him for his account being £2000 overdrawn.

'What?' he said.

She finished the chocolate and dropped the wrapper among the empty cans and pizza boxes on the floor.

'Self Esteem. Now she's great, telling the world how it really is. The sturdy girls have to stick together. Have you listened to *Some Fucking Wizadry*?' Kirby shook his head. 'Billy Nomates is another, just one woman and a tape deck with blistering lyrics.' She glanced at the pile of papers. 'Music has come a long way since I sat down with poor old Bobbie Johnson to talk about the blues.'

Kirby's heart thumped against his ribs, his chest threatening to burst as he gazed into her dark eyes.

'You're...?' He couldn't finish the sentence. Then she thrust her fingers towards him, and he noticed how her nails were perfect. He shook her hand, feeling her warmth transfer into him.

'You can call me Lucy.' She removed a mobile phone from her jacket. 'Now, is it the standard contract you want, or are you after something more personalised like I gave to Lennon?'

He waited for the ground to open up and swallow him, his mouth turning into a desert while a thousand angry flies buzzed inside his head. Kirby glanced at the papers and then the computer screen.

'But I didn't summon you.'

Her laugh made his spine crawl. 'Silly boy. Humans don't summon me.' She moved closer to him. 'I listen to what's in their dreams and hearts and offer my assistance to the chosen few. You're a fortunate young man.' She tapped on her phone. 'So, do you require my services or not?'

Kirby's heart had returned to normal as he spoke. 'What services?'

Lucy grinned at him, her teeth sparkling so white he thought she must be American.

'Your heart's desires, my boy, your heart's desires.'

His confidence was slowly returning to him. Maybe this was a joke played on him by Serena and James.

'And what do you get?'

Two small burning stars replaced her eyes, and he knew this wasn't a joke.

'You know what, Kirby.'

He took a deep breath. 'My soul?'

Lucy nodded. 'For all eternity. In return, I will give you your greatest desire, to be the most famous musician in the world, with millions of screaming souls at your feet. How does that sound?'

Kirby smiled at her. 'It sounds perfect, but I need one other thing?'

She returned his grin, and the hairs prickled on the back of his neck.

'Just name it.'

'I want you to torture and kill Serena and James.'

Lucy laughed. He watched tiny spiders fall from her sleeves and scuttle across his papers.

'My, my, what a wicked boy you are, Kirby Sigston.' She put one hand to her face, scratching at her cheek where he saw something slithering under her skin. 'Your proposal sounds lovely, but I don't get my hands dirty. You'll have to do that job yourself. It will be the final stamp on our contract, a sacrifice to seal the bond between us.'

'Two sacrifices,' he said.

She shrugged. 'Whatever.' She stuck her fingers out again. 'Do we have a contract?'

He took her hand, noticing how cold it was now. 'Where do I sign?'

Lucy let go of him. 'There's no signature needed in the modern age. Your handshake was enough. Once the sacrifice is complete, your part of the deal will take place. Do you understand?'

Kirby nodded, feeling the weight of the world finally lift from his shoulders.

'When should I do it?'

'That's up to you,' she said. 'But I'd suggest you check your email.'

He glanced from her to the computer, noticing the new messages. When he looked back, she'd vanished.

Had it all been a dream?

No. Kirby touched his palm, feeling how icy cold it was and remembering the blazing stars in her eyes. And he saw the tea cup with ruby lipstick on it. At least he assumed it was lipstick. He sat down and checked his emails, seeing one for a local outdoor music festival happening soon.

'Shit!' he said.

Two years ago, the three of them had bought tickets for the festival, but it was cancelled that year and last because of the pandemic. So he'd forgotten all about it until seeing the email. And the festival was only two weeks away.

He clicked on the message, scanning it before downloading the tickets.

'It would serve them right if I kept the tickets and sold them on.'

Then he had a better idea.

There would be thousands at the concert, a vast throng of people dancing at the front of the stage where anything could happen. And he knew how much Serena and James loved to be near the action.

He pushed his spine into the chair and gazed at the screen, glancing between the papers on the floor describing sacrifices and blood rituals and then back to the message.

Could he do it? Could he kill both of them at the festival, hidden inside the heaving bodies in the dark of the night?

Of course he could. He'd been slaughtering animals since he was a kid. Several dogs and cats had died at his hands, all the pets of the children who'd tormented him. And only last year, he'd slit that horse's throat, enjoying the feel of the blood on his fingers. If he could do those things, then killing Serena and James wouldn't be too much trouble. It would be a shame he couldn't torture them, but he'd leave that up to the Devil in Hell.

He laughed at the thought. Lucy in Hell. That was weird, seeing Satan as a woman.

Kirby pictured the pain and suffering they'd go through, those who'd betrayed him. Then, as he imagined their skin flayed from their bones, he emailed Serena their festival tickets, adding only a small message to it.

Perhaps I'll bump into you in the mosh pit.

Then he sat back, hoping the weeks would fly by.

They didn't. The waiting was misery for him, expecting Serena and James to return the tickets and tell him they weren't going.

'They're probably rehearsing their shitty synth music,' he said while watching torture videos. He knew the clips were all fake, but they excited him anyway.

He couldn't even distract himself by writing new songs because his brain was telling him it wouldn't matter – he didn't need to create anything now. Once he'd killed those two, Lucy would click her fingers, and she'd do everything for him. The only regret he had was not specifying to Satan what type of famous musician he wanted to be. From his research, he understood she would try to trick him somehow – for who would trust the Devil? – so she might make him a famous jazz musician or country rock star.

'Christ, she could turn me into the lead singer of a synth-pop duo.'

That thought made him laugh.

In the end, it didn't matter. He'd be happy if she made him rich and famous, and Serena and James suffered. Sure, he'd offered his soul to Lucy, but he figured he had probably another fifty years to live. There would be no rock and roll lifestyle for him, no quick death from excessive drinking and drugs. He'd have plenty of sex, but there would be no risks towards an early grave.

So, his only worry was how he would kill them at the concert. A knife seemed the easiest solution, stabbing them both quickly in the gut. Kirby had even checked the best way of doing it online, of the right organs to penetrate. He hadn't been stupid enough to use his computer for the search, stealing one from a punter in the goth club he frequented every Thursday night and using it to browse the web. He worried he might bump into Serena and James at the venue, but he hadn't.

The problem was how to get the knife past the security. They didn't have metal detectors, so he pictured strapping the blade to his chest or groin. But there was no need to worry in the end. After checking the early photos and comments of the festival goers on social media, he realised they didn't have enough guards to search everybody.

Kirby smiled when he read that, wondering if it was one of Lucy's manipulations.

He ate a hearty lunch at home before leaving. Shuttle busses were going to the venue from the market square, and

Kirby got one at five o'clock, giving him a few hours for a couple of drinks and to check the lay of the land. It would be dark by nine as the headline act came on stage, and he'd have plenty of time to find where James and Serena were. Both were heavy social media users, so locating them from their photos wouldn't be too difficult.

The knife was inside his jacket, safely sitting there since nobody at the gate had looked at anything apart from his ticket, which they swapped for a rainbow-coloured wristband. He kept touching it as he entered the grounds, knowing it would be a lovely memento of what he was about to do.

Yesterday's rain had left the ground damp and muddy in the parts where people had trod the most, mainly through the centre of the field and at the bars and toilets. The smell of the countryside filled the air, mixing in with the aromas from the food vendors dotted around the site.

Kirby bought a warm pint of cider in a reusable plastic cup, paying £2.50 for the container and twice as much for the alcohol. At least he could use the cup more than once. He sipped the booze and moved towards the main stage, dodging the kids running everywhere. It was a family-friendly music festival with good and bad points. The negative was avoiding the unruly children; the positive was smaller queues at the bars and the toilets. And far fewer drunken blokes were staggering around and pissing against the barriers.

He paused on the hill, watching the thousands ahead of him as a Dutch group entertained the audience. Kirby gripped his drink while checking his Instagram feed, seeing the latest photos posted by Serena and James. They were from ten minutes earlier, showing the loving couple smiling into the camera as the band played behind them. He looked away from the screen, searching for the point near the stage and confident he knew where it was. The day's last sunlight hovered above him, and he guessed it would be dark enough in thirty minutes for him to go unnoticed among the crowd.

The group played their final song, a raucous rock tune that got most of the crowd singing and dancing. The alcohol worked its way into Kirby's system, warming his insides and adding an extra fizz to the buzz that had grown inside him since he'd stepped beyond the gates. He finished the drink, contemplating getting another one, but decided against it if he wanted to keep a clear head for what was coming. The music ended, and he moved forward, peering at those around him, picking out the coolest t-shirts. Not the plethora of Ramones and Joy Divison shirts you saw at most gigs, mainly worn by people who hadn't been born when those two bands were around, but admiring the guy with the Nostromo shirt and grinning at the young woman wearing the Satan's Slaves top.

Lucy wants me to do this. She'll make sure I don't get caught.

He slipped the empty cup into his jacket, in the pocket opposite the blade. Then he rechecked his phone, not irritated anymore at the pictures of the two of them kissing. It wouldn't be long now, feeling the heat and frenzy of the horde growing around him.

The darkness descended in a rush, sweeping an ebony blanket over everything. Only the lights on the stage and from the screens of mobile phones illuminated the area. Then the crowd cheered as the headline act arrived. Kirby wasn't watching them; his eyes fixed on the couple a few feet in front of him, Serena and James wrapped in each other's arms.

Kirby reached into his jacket as electric guitars

screeched into life, and two sets of drums bashed out a beat that drowned out everything else. He gripped the knife, removing it under cover of darkness, close enough to Serena to smell the perfume that always drove him wild. Kirby could taste the blood in his mouth and hear the music vibrating inside his ears. Now he would get his revenge, and all his dreams would materialise.

And then Serena twisted around and smiled at him.

'We're glad you came, Kirby.'

Before he could reply, she grabbed the hand holding the knife. She squeezed his wrist, the pain shooting through him. Then she turned the blade on him and pushed it into his gut. It cut straight through his flimsy shirt and penetrated his skin. Serena twisted it from side to side, finding as many organs as possible. When she let go, the knife was buried deep in him.

'What?' he said.

She moved closer, kissing him on the lips and then moving back. The mass jostled around them, all unaware of what had happened.

'Lucy came to James and me, revealing what you'd done, how you wanted us tortured and murdered. So we made a better deal with her.' She grinned at him. 'We were always superior without you, Kirby.'

James grabbed her, and they vanished into the crowd. Kirby didn't move; his hands were pushed into his stomach and covered in blood. Nobody saw him. No one cared about him.

Then he fell backwards, crashing into the ground as kids ran around him, making fun of his name. The last thing he heard was the sound of an electronic keyboard and a cover version of Kraftwerk's *The Model* filling his head.

· · ·

The music had morphed into The Rolling Stones when he woke. The pain continued to sweep through Kirby as he looked up and realised he was on a stage. Red pinpricks of light flickered in the void in front of him, and he saw the crowd out there.

Then he heard them calling his name.

'Kirby, Kirby, Kirby, Kirby.'

On and on it went, sounding like adulation, but he knew it wasn't.

'They've been waiting for you.'

He turned to see Lucy standing there dressed as Ziggy Stardust.

'You cheated me,' he said.

She swung the guitar over her shoulder, and he noticed she had one foot on Sid Vicious's throat.

'Nope,' she said. 'I promised you a crowd of adoring millions, and you have them out there. But, unfortunately, adoration in Hell is not something you want to experience close up.'

They called his name again, and he felt warm urine running down his leg.

'You said I'd be the most famous musician in the world.'

Lucy put her arm around his shoulder. 'And you are, Kirby. This is my world, and I've told all my followers about you.' She dragged him to the edge of the stage. 'And they can't wait to meet you.'

The Necromancer's Diary

I was twelve years old when the dead visited me for the first time.

I'd had a terrible day at school, taunted by the other girls for the clothes I wore and the way I spoke. My father's death three months before had elicited little sympathy from my compatriots and had only increased my mother's dependency on the booze.

Retreating to my bedroom to bury myself in books and music was the only way I could escape from the torment around me. So on that fateful night, I'd stuck one of my father's Beatles albums into the CD player. My mother had wanted to throw all of his things away – she said it was her way of moving on – but I'd fought her on that.

I was still nursing the bruise below my eye when I noticed the temperature change in the room. It was a balmy summer's night, one of those where you leave all the windows open and kick the covers off as you struggle to sleep. Yet, my fingers shivered as the breath crawled from my lips and hung in the air as if I was smoking a cigarette.

I pressed a hand to my chest to find some warmth and

pushed away the plate of fries in my lap. The room had smelt of tomato ketchup, but now the aroma of rotten leaves lingered everywhere. The hairs stood on the back of my neck as I peered at the mist swirling near the window.

I'd left it open to cool the bedroom, but not like this. My legs trembled as I got off the bed, stepping towards the draft shimmering in front of me. Before the rest of me froze, the cold vapour transformed into a solid figure. The sound of electric guitars echoed through my ears as I reached for my throat and strangled the scream growing there. I fell back onto the bed and wondered if I'd eaten something terrible to make me hallucinate.

But no food could have made me see what I did that night: the mist disappeared, replaced by a withered old woman, with long matted grey hair, empty eyes, and a face looking as if hundreds of tiny meteorites had hit it.

I tried to tear my gaze from her but couldn't. She didn't appear to see me at first, craning her neck to peer above her. I followed her stare, wondering how the dark stain had got onto the bedroom ceiling.

Until it moved and I realised it wasn't a mark. The buzzing invaded my ears as the flies swarmed around each other. The group grew in size, and I couldn't see where they were coming from. My room stank like month-old rubbish as the insects stopped moving and the noise vanished. The only thing I could hear was the blood swimming through my veins and my heart thumping against my chest.

As I dug my nails into my palm, the ghost cranked her face towards the flies. Then the noise came again, of hundreds of legs rubbing against each other before they swept down and into her mouth. Her head grew bigger, like a balloon filling with water and ready to explode.

Blood dripped from my hand and onto the bed as she

turned to me. Her jaw moved up and down as she crunched on the insects and peered into my eyes. Then she swallowed them all, followed by a large burp that rattled the lights. Her arms and legs jerked to the side as she moved across the carpet like a demented puppet.

She staggered forward and put a hand on the wall. Her form was no longer made of mist but a physical form, wrinkled and yellow. I watched as she ran her fingers over the patterns in the wallpaper. There were cats and dogs on it, and when she touched them, they came to life before my eyes. They ran across the wallpaper, fighting each other, tearing throats out as I grabbed at mine. Their blood seeped into the walls and dripped onto the carpet. The lights flickered on and off, throwing a pink shade over the room, and making her move in and out of my vision.

Then she approached the bed.

Ice swam over my skin as she pointed a bony finger at me.

'John Lennon hates that song.'

Without me moving, the music doubled in volume and made the plastic figures of the Marvel characters wobble on the bookcase. They fell to the floor as the murderous animals in the wallpaper continued to rip each other to pieces. Their howling mixed in with the music. I put my hands over my ears, feeling the warmth of the blood in my palms. I was desperate to close my eyes but more afraid not to see the ghost than to observe her creeping towards me.

She reached out her arms, and they grew long enough to hover over my shoulders. Then, as I quivered below them, her head twisted out of shape, and I thought she was going to spew the flies at me.

Then my mother barged through the door to complain about the noise.

'Turn that down, Caroline,' she shouted at me.

I came out of my frozen state, ready to tell her about the ghost in the room, but the old woman had vanished, leaving behind a wicked grin reminiscent of the Cheshire cat. It loitered a few inches above me for a few seconds before following the rest of her.

My mother turned off the music before launching into a tirade of insults at her only child. I sat there and stared at the normality of the wallpaper. Then I glanced down to see the blood had disappeared from the carpet, and I wondered if I'd dreamt the whole thing.

But I hadn't.

After that day, the departed kept coming, and I couldn't do anything about it.

I'd never been able to figure out how I'd done it the first time, summoning the spirit of the old woman into my bedroom twenty years ago, but bringing the dead to me nowadays was as easy as changing the channel on the TV.

Yet, even with two decades of experience and knowledge, summoning the dead was not without its risks. For example, if I attempted it in the wrong location, I might end up with more of the deceased than I'd bargained for. Moreover, a spirit dragged out of its deathly state was rarely happy about the change in its circumstances. And an angry ghost usually turned into a violent one: the scars on my body were testament to that.

It took me twenty years before I got complete control of my "gift", and all the trials and tribulations I went through were finally worth it when I turned the dead into a money-making scheme.

The arrival of the internet made everything easier in my business as a necromancer. Without it, I would never have reached so many clients or received the payments quickly and safely. Even with that, I still took every precaution to protect myself, which was why I was trudging through the snow to the hotel I'd booked the week before. Once I'd received the details and deposit from my latest client, I'd picked the best place for the meeting, choosing somewhere well away from prying ears and eyes.

And as far away from a cemetery or morgue as possible.

The snow had been falling since the early hours of the morning. As I peered through it at the hotel sign, the flakes appeared to shimmer with a deathly hallow. The wind flickered around my head as I stepped into the building and checked in to my first-floor room. I dumped my small bag on the bed and went out for something to eat.

I headed to the nearest pub, hoping it was a new build and not one which had been around for centuries. But I was out of luck. The older the building, the more likely I'd encounter at least one wandering spirit. Even when I wasn't calling them back to the mortal world, I could still see some of them around me, lingering in the places they'd died.

And the more violent the death, the more chance there would be of me bumping into them. Things that go bump in the night was only half true because ghosts could appear at any time of the day. And bumping was the correct term to use because once they'd passed through their misty phase, they could become as solid as any human.

I had one glass of wine with some pasta, ignoring the things only I could see. The staff got on with their work while what few customers were there enjoyed themselves. The ghosts of children were always the most painful to see, and one had come to a violent death on that spot in the last fifty years. She didn't approach me, loitering near the bar and peering at the wall.

In the early days of the necromancer's life, I would

speak to children like this, thinking I could bring some form of peace to them, but it never worked. Half the time, I'd only make things worse. Some spirits don't realise they're dead until they encounter someone like me. And that realisation is a terrible thing to see.

When the girl in the pub had started crying tears only I could hear, I paid my bill and returned to my room. I looked at the neon clock on the wall to see ten minutes before the client would arrive. I removed my coat and hung it on the back of a chair before going into the bathroom. Inside, I peered at my reflection in the mirror and instantly disliked what I saw. It wasn't that I thought I was unattractive, even though I'd long stopped caring about such things. When you spend most of your life staring at the dead, you soon realise the superficiality of appearance is one less thing to worry about in your daily existence.

No, what I didn't like about my face, what I'd never liked, was how much I resembled my mother. How could I be happy to see the woman who had beaten me every day staring back at me, even though she'd been dead for ten years?

I'd tried many things to change my appearance, from drastic haircuts and unusual hair dyes to using different coloured contact lenses and even caking my skin in too much makeup. But nothing could ever change what I saw in my reflection.

The only good thing my mother ever taught me was how to get fake passports and credit cards. She managed to pass on to me the lessons she'd learnt during her time inside the prison system without me ever having to experience the same thing. However, I always assumed living with her was not too dissimilar to being locked up with a bunch of psychopaths. At least there was only one of her, but that was enough.

I splashed water over my face and returned to the other room. I went to my bag and removed what I needed for the ceremony, placing them on the bed to ensure I had everything. Once, ten years ago, I'd forgotten to bring the phial of lamb's blood with me. When I'd tried to explain to the client, a fifty-year-old builder who'd lost his wife six months previously, that I would have to rearrange the summoning, he'd dropped to his knees and begged me to go through with it. I'd peered into his bloodshot eyes and guessed he must have thought I was a charlatan about to disappear with his money. Then he'd told me that twice before that night, other so-called necromancers had taken his money without bringing his dead wife back to him.

'It's not a resurrection,' I'd told him as he cried into the carpet.

'I know,' he'd said. 'I just want the chance to say goodbye to her.' His wife had died of a stroke while he was at work. She was forty-two years old when she'd passed away, without any previous health issues.

I told him again I couldn't do anything without the right amount of blood.

That's when he rolled up his sleeve and stuck his arm out to me.

'Take mine.' He dug a long nail into his skin and cut across it. 'Take as much as you want.'

Against my better judgement, I did as he pleaded.

And that's when it all went wrong.

I pushed the memory from my mind when there was a knock on the door.

I opened it to see a tall woman, dressed in a black jacket and trousers, wearing brown high-heeled shoes, making her seem even taller. Around her throat was a blood-red scarf, contrasting vividly with her pale skin. It was nearly midnight, but she was wearing dark glasses.

'Are you Caz Maston, the necromancer?'

She could have been anywhere between twenty and thirty, and her voice did nothing to give her age away.

'Take off your glasses.' I said.

There were photographs of the client on my phone, along with personal details she'd given me as well as others she hadn't. I'd made many mistakes in the early days of my necromancy, but I'd learnt valuable lessons from them all. And the most important was to do a thorough background check of everyone who wanted me to bring the dead to them.

She removed the glasses, and I stared at the woman from the photos: Susie Stax.

'Can I come in?' Listening to her voice was like sucking on an ice cube during a storm.

I stood to the side, and she entered. As I closed the door, I watched her scan the room as if she was an escaped convict. Then she turned to me.

'You got the first payment?'

I nodded as I took my phone from my pocket. 'If you send the rest now, I'll get on with the summoning.'

Nothing moved but her eyes, still searching the room before settling on what I'd laid on the bed.

'I thought the rite had to be performed around a pit with fire during nocturnal hours, using a specific recipe, which includes the blood of sacrificial animals, to concoct a libation for the ghosts to drink while you recite prayers to both the ghosts and gods of the underworld?'

My smile made my lips feel even drier than they were. 'Well, I've turned the heating up, it's gone midnight, and

I've got the blood. The prayers are all in my head, but I still need something from you. I mentioned this to you online.'

Susie reached inside her jacket.

A silent sigh crept out of me as she removed a necklace and handed it to me.

'Our parents gave Emma and me identical necklaces on our fourteenth birthday.'

I didn't take it from her. 'You were identical twins?'

She nodded. 'Yes. Until she disappeared and left only this behind.'

Susie had told me all of this online, but I needed to hear it from her. 'You found the necklace near the river?'

'The woods weren't far from our house. We'd been there many times, but this was the first time we'd gone there for a drink.' Her eyes glazed over. 'It was my idea to get the cider.'

'How did you get it?'

She placed her free hand next to her leg. It must have been to hide the shaking in her fingers, but it didn't work.

'I had an older boyfriend who got it for me. He thought I'd meet him on the industrial estate, but Emma talked me into taking it into the woods for us to celebrate turning fourteen.'

Her head dipped as she pushed the necklace closer to me. I took it from her and felt its chill.

'The police never found your sister?'

She moved closer to me and pushed the hair from her right eye, revealing a large scar on her forehead.

'There was a noise behind me. When I turned around, someone hit me on the head, knocking me out. When I woke, Emma was gone, with her necklace on the edge of the river.'

I'd checked her story online. It was big news at the time

but had slipped into the forgotten realms of the internet over the years. The police had dragged the water, but after finding no trace of Emma there or in the woods, things were scaled down a few weeks later before eventually being pushed into a cold case file.

'The police questioned your boyfriend about Emma's disappearance.'

Her eyes sank into her cheeks. 'They did. The police found bits of the cider bottle near where I woke up, and they had Charlie's fingerprints on them.'

'Wasn't that because he bought the cider for you?'

Susie rubbed at her face. 'That's what I told them.' She let out a heavy sigh. 'They released him eventually, but it didn't matter to some people. They still believed he was involved somehow.'

'But you didn't?'

'No. Charlie was the gentlest person I ever met. He couldn't harm a fly.'

'Did you stay in touch with him?'

She shook her head. 'Not for long. He moved away six months after Emma's disappearance. I think his family couldn't take any more of the hassle. After that, we lost touch, and I don't know what happened to Charlie.'

But I did. He'd changed his surname, so it was tricky to track him down, but it wasn't too difficult once I discovered he had a police record. Charlie Cross was in and out of prison for what some would call petty thefts between the ages of eighteen and thirty. That was until he was found hanging in his cell not long after his thirtieth birthday. The coroner classed it as suicide, but Charlie's family claimed he was murdered.

Contrary to what she'd said, I wondered if Susie knew any of that as I asked her a different question.

'What makes you think your sister's dead?'

Susie Stax shook her head. 'What else could it be? Emma wouldn't have run away. She would have got in touch with me, somehow. I know it.'

'So that's why you contacted me?'

Her fingers stopped shaking as she laughed. 'Your reviews on the dark web are impressive.' She took out her phone and tapped on the screen for a minute. 'I've sent you the final payment if you want to check it.'

I moved to the bed. 'I trust you, Susie.' I picked up the phial of lamb's blood and the bowl to pour it in. 'Are you sure you still want to do this?'

She nodded. 'I have to know what happened to my sister.'

I placed the bowl on the floor between us and poured the blood into it. The smell of burnt copper lingered in the air as I put the necklace over the liquid. Then I placed it into the blood. As Susie Stax peered at me, I ran through the mantra inside my head. It was no ancient, mystical spell but the lyrics to *Five Years* by David Bowie.

By the time Bowie was peering into an ice-cream parlour, the temperature had dropped, so Susie was trembling again. Then, behind her, the air shimmered, and that familiar mist appeared in the room. I reached out to pull her towards me, but she must have felt the change happening over her shoulder.

She stumbled into me as she turned. 'Is that...that...that her?'

It was hard to tell at that point. The ghostly form was still mostly mist, with no discernible human appearance.

Then the legs came first, followed by arms, the torso, and finally the head. Stax was frozen next to me, but there was no doubt who the ghost was.

'Don't move until she speaks,' I said.

We stood there in silence as the smell of leaves floating in the water filled the room.

Susie pulled away from me, with her foot kicking into the side of the blood bowl, as she ignored my advice.

'Emma, is that you?'

The ghost floated towards us, raising one pale hand to move the hair from her face. Susie gasped at the sight, but I was unsurprised at what I saw: damp, dark leaves clung to Emma Stax's cheeks, above which were two burning red pinpricks where her eyes should have been. Her lips were blacker than the night and trembled as she spoke.

'Why have you brought me here, Susie?'

Susie clutched at her heart. 'I had to know what happened to you.'

The ghost of Emma Stax smiled, and even with my twenty years of experience with the dead, my skin crawled at the sight. She opened her lips again, ready to speak before a pile of worms fell from her mouth and onto the carpet.

'You know what happened to me, sister. You always have done.'

Susie dropped to her knees, the only noise in the room being her heavy sobbing. Then she thrust her hand into the blood and removed the necklace from it. She bent her face into it before pulling up in a jerk. I peered at the blood on her skin as Emma Stax thrust out a ghostly arm.

Susie stood and reached out for her dead twin sister.

I tried to pull her back, knowing how catastrophic it could be when the living and the dead come together. But, before I could, the ghost of Emma Stax disappeared back to wherever it had come from.

Susie turned to me. 'It was an accident. You have to believe me.'

'You argued with your sister and pushed her into the river?'

She wiped blood and tears from her eyes. 'She wanted to drink more of the cider, but I wouldn't let her. We were both already drunk, and she grabbed the bottle from me. We fought over it, and Emma hit me in the head with it. That's when I shoved her into the water. I blacked out after that.'

Had she forgotten all of this, only for her memories to reawaken when seeing her sister's ghost? Or had she known it all along, even before she'd come here tonight?

And how much more was she still keeping to herself? Why didn't the police find the body in the river if it had happened, as she said? Was she lying to me? Perhaps it wasn't an accident, and she'd killed Emma and then disposed of her body.

Did I want to know the answer to these questions?

In my line of work, I have no friends. So there is nobody for me to confide in, but if there were, I'd guess one of the first questions they'd ask would be why I do what I do.

And my answer would be: I'm here to help the living with their grief.

I watched Susie Stax wipe the blood from the necklace and put it into her pocket. I couldn't tell if the look on her face was one of grief, guilt, or regret.

Or perhaps it was a combination of all three.

She didn't speak as she left. I packed my things away and peered at the bed.

Then I turned on the TV and searched through all the channels to find something funny to watch.

As I settled down to watch an episode of *Father Ted*, the two red pinpricks in the corner of the room finally disappeared.

The Island of Lost Souls

Peering at a corpse was as jarring as you might expect. Two added facts made it weirder: I was floating six feet above the deceased, hovering like a car glued to a giant magnet before being crushed. However, as strange as that was, it didn't bother me as much as the realisation the body below me was mine.

The rest of the school ran to my stricken frame, fingers raised to open mouths at the sight of life trickling from my head. I was incorporeal, but somehow I smelt the bouquet of blood mixed in with the sweat of teachers and students. I turned my ghostly face to the stage, remembering how I'd taken a wrong step and missed the edge, tumbling to the floor below.

It was to have been my finest hour, a presentation on the paradoxes and idiosyncrasies of probability. And now, the only paradox concerning me was how I ended up as a spectre of my former self. I was the mathematics star, destined for one of the country's highest academic or government posts.

But not anymore.

As I wondered what to do next, the choice was taken from me. The school disappeared, and I landed somewhere hard with a bump. I stood on flat land that appeared to go into infinity. There was nothing but a shimmering mist and a pale imitation of the sky above me. I scanned the area and saw a grey desert with a haze swirling around.

'The Island of Lost Souls is bigger than you could imagine.'

The voice was splintered rocks brushed against shattered glass. A creature shaped like a giant football pushed through the vapour. Resting on top of its spherical torso was a misshapen head straight from Hieronymus Bosch, all of its features out of place and in constant motion. It moved on six spidery legs scuttling towards me.

'Where am I?' I stood unblinking and defiant in front of this thing from a terrible, twisted nightmare.

'I mean you no harm, Chloe. My name is Alan, and I'm here to guide you through the Island.'

'How do you know who I am?' I found that stranger than the fact I was dead. 'And what are you?'

Alan's eyes whirled around his face like watery eggs on the wrong parts of his head before settling down and peering at me.

'The longer the human body stays on the Island of Lost Souls, the more messed up it gets.' His lips bubbled up and down, revealing a mouth missing half its teeth. 'And as the guide here, I know every soul who arrives.'

'You're human?' My voice trembled.

'I was once.'

'Why am I here?'

Alan bounced up and down like an agitated child, his

spidery legs threatening to snap under the exertion. His football-shaped torso spun around and around under his head, and I wanted to throw up.

'You're here while a decision is taken on your final destination.'

I pointed towards his constantly changing face. 'Can you stop doing that, please?'

His eyes settled into their normal spot, and his stomach stopped moving. That's when I noticed he had tiny, spindly arms twitching at either side of his bulbous torso.

'Sorry,' he said.

A noise in the distance distracted me. 'What else is here?' The scrambled eggs I had for breakfast were dancing through my guts.

Alan rolled around like a distorted balloon, ready to pop. 'All the souls of humanity not yet in the Light or the Darkness are here. You're Lost until you're Found. If you stay here too long, those living inside the mist will feast on you for all eternity.'

The thought of eating anything twisted my stomach as the screaming moved closer. I stared into the air while I spoke to Alan.

'Who decides where I'll go?'

'Your fate rests on a gamble, on a wager for your eternal soul.' The thing which was Alan's mouth turned inside out, and worms wriggled on its tongue. I stopped myself from gagging with a hand over my lips.

The screeching hurt my ears. 'Do you know what that noise is?'

His eyes swirled around again. His tiny, twitching fingers pointed into the haze above our heads. 'The Collectors are here for you. We must move now.'

It was a piercing shriek that shattered the mist. Then I saw them coming for me. Haggard-faced and wild-haired, their teeth bared, and spears clutched in their yellowed hands.

Alan's spindly arm was stronger than it looked. He threw me over his malformed back and sped away from the horror. He rolled into the vapour as a spear brushed my leg and buried itself in the dirt. The environment swallowed us, my guide travelling at a pace that meant the noises were soon in the distance.

Sometime later, we stopped. He deposited me at the side of a vast lake, waving his fingers at me. 'Don't fall into the river; there are worse things there than the Collectors.'

I spat dirt from my mouth, the smell of saltwater bursting into my brain, peering into the horizon. A great shadow drifted over the water. 'What's that?'

'It's the misery of the damned.' His eyes dropped to either side of his nose. Each time I glanced at him, it hurt my head.

I strode nearer to the edge of the river; shapes twisted beneath it, shadows which swam and slithered under the liquid. I didn't want to know what they were.

The shadow was a ship approaching, with thousands of people on board. Desperate humanity crammed into every space. They screamed at me, their heads contorted, exhibiting a fitful terror. Their faces were wide, gaunt and harsh, trembling fingers clutching at sallow cheeks and bulging eyes, pulling out hair and weeping.

'What is this?' I looked into Alan's strange appearance.

'They're the ones who lost their gamble.'

'Where's it going?' The horror ship sailed past us. Some wailing bodies threw themselves over the side, only to get caught in large nets made from wide-mouthed rats biting at the humans in their grasp.

'Its final destination is the Darkness.'

I turned from the seething masses. 'Where are you taking me?'

He skittered to my side, his feet bouncing off the ground. More shrieks were in the air, those horrors from earlier hovering above us. They moved from side to side, up and down like a murmuration of starlings.

'You're already here.'

The mist covered me, swirling into my ears, up my nose, and over my eyes. I was sightless, struggling to breathe, clutching my throat when the haze dissipated, and I fell to my knees. Alan and everything else disappeared.

I was in a different place now.

I stood and wiped the dirt from my cheeks. Looming ahead was a towering gothic building. Its brickwork was scorched red, the top reaching so far into the sky I couldn't see the end. Something told me to enter. I opened the door and marched inside. A woman sat at a table, her face like an exploding sun.

'You took a fine time getting here, Chloe; did you get lost?'

'I fell off a stage.'

Playing cards was in her hands. 'Yes, that was an accident.' She shuffled the pack and pointed to sit opposite her.

I slipped into the chair. 'Why am I here?'

That grin continued to dazzle. 'My name is Lucy, and I have a wager for you.'

'What wager?'

She placed the cards on the table. 'We have one round of poker, you against me. If you win, you can return to your Earthly frame or move on into the Light.'

'What happens if I lose?'

Her smile was as bright as a morning star. 'You accompany me into the Darkness.'

'I've never played the game before; this wouldn't be fair.'

Lucy stroked her chin and considered my words. 'I'll play a few hands with friends, and you can watch and study. You're the brightest in your school, a whizz at maths and science; this should be a doddle for you.' She scratched a nail into the table. 'And it's the only concession I'll give you.'

What choice did I have? 'Okay.'

She waved her fingers, and two skeletons appeared on either side. 'These are my regular poker partners; you'll learn much from them.'

They played six rounds, with Lucy winning every time. After each hand, the cards were flipped over and returned unshuffled to the bottom of the pack. Her eyes sparkled as she peered at me, and the skeletons vanished. She dealt again.

I looked at mine. 'I'll take one.' I discarded a king face down.

Lucy pushed it to the side. 'I'll keep what I have.' She placed hers on the table and turned them over all at once, a single queen surrounded by four aces.

I flipped over my cards one at a time to reveal a straight run from six to ten. Watching the blood boil in her cheeks was interesting.

'How did you do that?'

I got up from my chair. 'I choose to live again. Will you send me back?'

Steam flew from her ears as she waved a hand in my

face, and I vanished from the Island of Lost Souls. I reappeared in the school, my foot close to falling off the stage.

'Are you okay, Chloe?' The maths teacher, Mr Arnold, stared at me. 'Can you continue with your presentation?'

I grinned at him. 'I will, sir.'

All I had to do was clear my mind of the cards I'd counted.

The Shadow

I: Rose's Story

I stood outside the high-rise when the woman jumped from the tenth-floor window.

The flats loomed over me, casting shadows that joined the wind and cut into my bones. I'd never enjoyed visiting the place, only going because my mother had dragged me to see Grandma. Gran was losing the plot, and I hated seeing her in that state of her forgetting who she was and struggling to look after herself. After a fall last Christmas had left Gran with two fractured ribs, Mum had arranged for carers to visit Gran three times a day. Mum would still go at least once a week, but I avoided it if I could.

I was only there that day because I'd read online that Zoe, the Instagram Influencer, was shooting an advert across the road near the Prince statue. No matter how hard I tried, I couldn't find an answer to why there was a Prince statue in the middle of a council estate in the north of England, but it was cool to see it.

My ambition was to become that famous I'd be like those stars who only used one name — like Zoe and Prince. My mother said an eighteen-year-old shouldn't be wasting their time on stupid dreams, but what's the point of having an ambition if you don't shoot for the stars?

Anyway, that's why I was there the morning that woman jumped from the window.

Mum was already walking towards the entrance of the flats when I saw the group around the Prince statue — teenagers carrying red balloons and people dressed as clowns. There was music playing, but I couldn't make out what it was. I was straining my ears to hear it when I heard the shouting from above me. That's when I looked up to see the woman hanging out of the window.

'Hey, you, girl! Girl!'

The pleading in her voice made me tremble. It was a bright summer day, the sun on my face and the smell of candy floss coming from somewhere. But the sound of that voice sent a shiver through me.

'Hey, girl! Girl!'

Mum was already in the building, and the clowns were boogieing in the road, stopping the cars from moving and drawing angry shouts from the drivers. Then, from the edge of my vision, I saw a uniformed copper trying to calm everything down as the teenagers released their balloons into the air.

'Hey, you, girl!'

Her words were like an anchor in my head while my body was the *Titanic*. I moved closer to the building and gazed at her.

'Girl, you've got to get me out of here.'

'Rose, what are you doing?'

Mum's voice shook my attention away from the woman in the window. By the time I glanced back up, she'd gone.

That's when I heard the body hit the ground.

It was the sound of a tomato sauce bottle squeezed of its last snort, a colossal splat that made me fear the worse when I opened my eyes to look at the damage.

But she was lying there untouched.

I held my breath, ready to run to her, when something made me stop.

No, not something — it: the shadow.

I thought at first it was from something else, maybe a shadow from the building until I realised it was crawling from her body. Not from underneath or behind her, but from *inside* her. Shadowy hands with long fingers came out, digging dark nails into the pavement and dragging the shape from the body. I wanted to turn and run, but my legs were frozen, rooted to that spot as dozens of red balloons floated past me.

But maybe it was all in my head. What if the woman was still alive?

Then, as the shadow was finally out of her, the thing twisted its head at me and grinned. I'm not sure how it happened, but the mouth and eyes — Jesus, those eyes — were lighter than the rest of it.

And it gazed straight at me. Then, grinning with sharp shadow teeth, its long fingers dug into the pavement, and it crawled towards me.

I can't remember anything after that.

II: Kara's Story

Rose isn't a bad child. She's my only daughter, and I'm as proud as hell of her, but she gets some strange notions in her head sometimes. Still, I guess it's the same with most teenagers nowadays — wanting to be internet stars and famous for doing nothing at all. She's obsessed with social media, YouTube, TikTok, and God knows what else I don't know about. I thought about taking the phone from her, but how could I? She'd report me to social services for cruelty.

It was different in my day. We never had access to the fancy stuff kids have now. And my mother would never have let me have the things that Rose has.

My mother.

That's why we were there that morning, completing my duties for the woman who'd never loved me. But what could I do? I'm not one of those horrible children who abandon their parents when things go wrong for them.

And they'd been going wrong for a while, with dementia and everything that it brought with it: memory loss, agitated behaviour, incontinence, and nearly burning down her flat.

Therefore, every visit to my mother was stressful. That's why I was focused on her when I walked into the building without realising Rose wasn't with me. I was halfway to the lifts when I noticed her absence. So I was angry when I went back outside and saw her just standing there like an idiot, gawping into the sky. At first, I thought she was staring at those balloons, and a clown fighting with a copper in the street distracted me.

Then I saw the body hit the ground only a few feet from me.

My God, the noise it made — like a car hitting some-body at sixty miles an hour. I clutched at my throat, about to throw up when I had this horrible thought: what if they'd fallen onto Rose?

I stumbled forward, expecting to see blood and bones everywhere, but there was only the body.

Then I saw Rose staring at the dead woman. And relief overwhelmed me. She was in shock; I could tell by her face, but who wouldn't be? I was about to go around the body and run to her when something moved between us. Another mad idea swept through me that the woman was still alive. Perhaps she'd only fallen from the first or second floor. That would explain why there was no blood.

But what I saw was more impossible than that.

It was a shadow crawling from the body.

I gasped. 'What?'

Then the thing jerked its head back to stare at me through black holes for eyes. And they were dragging me towards them. My legs refused to shift as the creature grinned at me.

It grinned at me!

Thick glue smothered the inside of my head, squeezing the life from my brain. I saw Rose's mouth tremble, but the only thing I heard were those clowns blowing their stupid horns. Then there was another sound from above me. I twisted my neck, seeing a man leaning out of a window near the top of the building and staring at me.

No, he wasn't looking at me but at that moving shadow.

He shouted something. I couldn't hear it, but the noise unfroze my brain and legs. I ran forward, jumping over the corpse, ready to fight the thing that was threatening my daughter.

But it was gone.

I threw my arms around Rose and hugged her. She was

cold and unmoving, but I felt her heartbeat next to mine. We stood like that until I heard the ambulance coming down the street.

III: Jack's Story

I was halfway through a twelve-hour shift when we got the call to go to the Greenway flats. I knew how serious it was because the ambulance service categorises all the calls it gets. Category one is the most life-threatening and needs to be attended to within seven minutes. Category four have a response time of three hours. So although most people think every day on an ambulance is different, there are typical jobs you'll be called to daily.

The first job of that morning was an older man who'd fallen in his flat. He'd been on the carpet all night until his carer found him on their visit. He was okay when we arrived, so we lifted him off the floor and got him comfortable. Then I made him some tea and toast, and we had a chat.

After that, we received a "birth imminent" message. We arrived there to find a woman giving birth on her bathroom floor. We asked for extra resources straight away as we delivered the baby at home. Mum and dad were both first-time parents and required a lot of reassurance. But, within five minutes, the child was born, and she was fine.

As I ensured that mother and child were okay, we received another call for a category one. The incident was two minutes from us, so we left the new parents and went to Greenway flats. Yet, something strange happened then. We got another message saying there was some confusion about whether or not the person was alive — there was a report of somebody falling from a high rise, but they were still moving on the ground.

I processed that information when we approached the scene, dodging a fight in the middle of the road between a uniformed police officer and a clown. We parked outside the flats, jumping out of the ambulance and seeing the body on the ground. Even from where I was, I could tell they couldn't be alive — the amount of blood staining the street made that obvious.

Apart from the clown and the copper screaming at each other, the place was silent. I was moving towards the body when I saw two women standing in front of me, unmoving and in shock. As I got closer and saw their faces, it was apparent they must be mother and daughter. My partner rushed past me to the body. I should have joined him, but something strange stopped me: a long shadow between the mother and daughter.

And it was moving.

I couldn't believe what I was seeing. The shadow slithered like a snake between the women, crawling up the older woman's leg before sliding onto the daughter. It kept doing that, going back and forth between them as I stood there transfixed.

'There's nothing we can do here, Jack,' my partner shouted at me. 'You better see if those two women are okay.'

He was right. There was nothing wrong with my legs, but my brain wouldn't let me move. The slithering shadow made my skin crawl, but then it got worse.

It had a head with a face.

And it smiled at me.

I'm ashamed to say it, but when I saw that grin, I pissed myself.

Warm urine slid down my leg, came out of my trousers,

and created a stinking yellow pool on the pavement. The smell flicked a trigger in my brain, and I was ready to move.

Until I heard a voice.

It's voice.

The shadow.

Don't go, Jack. You'll be my vessel. It's been such a long time since I've lived inside a male human. These women are too feeble for my tastes, lacking the strength for what I'll do. But you're stronger; I see that in your mind. All the terrible things you've seen and experienced will make you the perfect partner for me. All you have to do is step forward, and a great new world can be yours.

My feet moved without me telling them to, reaching out a hand for the shadowy black fingers creeping towards me.

And I was ready for them, hungry to feel their touch.

That was until a clown barged into me.

IV: Bob's Story

You never know what you'll run up against when working as a clown. I mean, some people have the craziest expectations. To be a professional clown takes commitment and sacrifice beyond what the public sees. It's hard work and not for everyone. The public sees only about twenty per cent of what goes into working in the profession. As a professional clown, you have to perform even when it's difficult, such as if you're ill or injured. It sounds extreme, but it goes with the territory. Unfortunately, most people aren't up to the challenge. In the old days, you got called a trouper for this.

And I'm a trouper.

I've done double duty as a traditional clown and any

number of costumed characters — whatever the client asks for — including the Cat In The Hat, Batman, a Squid Game thug, even the latest prime minister. And the situations can get hairy. For example, at one adult party, where I dressed as a Tarzan clown, some granny kept grinding against me, asking if she could spank my monkey.

Most of my work is for an agency, where you're sent out in pairs or groups. And there's a lot of female clowns in the industry now, so clowncest is a regular thing. If you've ever wanted to see what it looks like when nightmares breed, hang around a clown's car after a performance. Heck, I was once hired for a Halloween shindig, dressed as Pennywise, the clown from Stephen King's *It*. I spent most of it avoiding a female Freddy Krueger lookalike trying to rip my clothes off.

So I've seen some strange and terrifying things in my time working as a clown, but that day beats the lot.

First, I turned up with the other clowns for some woman's Instagram promotion party. I couldn't remember her name, and it paid peanuts. But, damn, if anyone's a clown, it's those people influenced by wannabes on social media. But, and this happens often, we could sample the booze on offer. This meant most of the other Bozos and I were pretty merry before the copper turned up to tell us to turn the noise down.

It was too late by then, but I'm not sure how I was the one who ended up fighting with the boy in blue in the middle of the road. I guess that's how I missed the drama of the woman jumping from the tenth floor of those flats. Even the copper can't have seen it, or he wouldn't have continued scrapping with me. When the ambulance came screaming around the corner, I thought that might have stopped him from pounding on me, but he must have had some childhood trauma with a clown, considering how angry he was.

Still, I didn't mind the bust-up — it was better than having to listen to the Instagram woman going on and on about her stupid career. Her voice was liquid Valium, calming to the point of comatose, with each word she spoke more meaningless than the one before. By the end of a sentence, I was far worse informed than if she'd said nothing. Instead of wasting time on the internet entertaining morons, her ideal job would have been as a doctor specialising in telling patients their cancer was now terminal. Because everyone would have either nodded off or died before they'd absorbed the news.

So, it hadn't been a good day until I got into an argument with the copper, apart from the free booze. Then, as the ambulance swerved past us and the police officer let go of me, I stumbled back and saw two women standing in front of the body.

But it was what I saw next that scared the shit out of me — a black, slithering snake crawling over the women. Now, I hate snakes at the best of times, so I was glad when I realised it wasn't one of those slimy bastards.

That was until I understood what it was — a living shadow.

It had a head and face and mouth, and fuck me if the whole of my body was screaming at me to run. I saw it crawl all over those two women, that sight making the alcohol turn into bile in my throat. Then it crept away from them and slithered towards a paramedic from the ambulance. I expected him to shout and scream, but he just stood there.

And that's when I heard the voice.

The shadow was speaking inside my head, a terrible, flesh-crawling sound that made me bend over and throw up.

The vomit stink assaulted my senses, but it didn't stop me from hearing that voice.

My God, that voice. I can still hear it now.

But then, outside that building, the copper jumped on me, and we went flying into the paramedic, with all three of us ending up on the ground.

My head was on the pavement when I saw the shadow slithering towards us.

V: Terry's Story

I had no choice. I threw Sally out of the window.

Thirty years together, and none of it was good. It wasn't how I'd expected things to be when I reached fifty, having to listen to her talking to that imaginary thing in her head. But, even when I punished her, it never went away. Starving her was good for Sally because she lost all that weight. And when I stopped her from watching all those terrible TV shows, she couldn't admit it was better for her. I mean, which intelligent person spends their time watching *Gogglebox* and *The Crown*. And when she wasn't doing that, Sally was reading trash like *The Da Vinci Code* or *Fifty Shades of Grey*. I wouldn't have minded if she'd been like the woman in that book, but she was never interested in sex. Because of her beliefs, I thought she was saving herself for after the marriage, but I was fooling myself.

So I guess it was Sally's fault I had to get the strap out and lock her away.

I blame it on her upbringing. I never liked her parents, and I know the feeling was mutual. Sally told me what it was like for her as a kid, how her mum and dad built her daily life around a church schedule: catechism classes every

Wednesday, which her parents taught. Thursday afternoons were for altar server practice. Confessions were on Saturdays, which she couldn't miss, or else she'd be forbidden from Sunday communion.

Her relationship with God was more important than her career, well-being, education, and family. And it was more important than our marriage. And because of the voice in her head, Sally's parents convinced her of the thing that eventually destroyed us.

'The voice in my head is a demon,' she told me the day after our wedding. 'And it has possessed me my entire life.'

I didn't believe her at first, thinking she was using it as an excuse to defy me. But even after I punished her, she never changed her story. And she was always talking to that other voice.

'I have to,' she said. 'If I don't, it will control me, and it wants me to do terrible things.'

'What terrible things?' I said.

She wouldn't tell me at first, but she wilted once I took the strap to her back.

'It tells me to kill people,' Sally said. 'To torture them first, but then kill lots of people. It screams at me every minute of the day to do these things.' I knew she was mad then. 'And most of all, it wants me to kill you.'

By then, I'd stopped listening to her protests against me touching her. So instead, I did what I wanted, when I wanted. And I never let her out of the flat. I'd wondered why she never complained or fought back against the imprisonment. When I was at work, I had to make sure she couldn't get out, but she could have shouted to a neighbour. Or even opened that window I pushed her out of to call for help.

Then I understood why she hadn't attempted to leave me — if she was imprisoned in that flat, so was the demon.

So it was good for a long time. Her strict upbringing had taught her to be subservient to her husband, so I got everything I wanted. I didn't need to use force then, but I enjoyed doing it every once in a while.

But then I met somebody else — and it was in the same block of flats. She was rich, a wealthy widow. Divorce was out of the question — Sally would never have agreed to it, no matter how much I beat her.

So she had to go out of the window.

Even before she went, I think she knew it was better for her as well. At least the demon would be gone then.

Yes, it was a good thing for everybody all around.

VI: The Shadow's Story

I've lived more than a thousand lives.

All I have to do is crawl under the skin and settle into that heart. Once I'm inside, and my dark fingers are massaging those four chambers, there's no way to get rid of me. I can sneak into any human — it's impossible to stop me — but the perfect vessel is a newborn child. Then I live in the heart and grow with it. I have no control over them then because the body is too young, but my strength and power increase as the baby grows. Slithering into an adult is quicker, but they can deny my influence if their will is strong.

And it's never as satisfactory as controlling a child and growing with them. It's a slow process, like hibernation, but worth it. It's different in every child, but complete control usually comes around the age of six or seven.

I'd waited in that hospital for too long, trying to find the perfect family. It's essential to get the right parents — you don't want the ones who smother their kids with love. Hate fuels me, and I need it early on when the vessel is young. So it has to be a mother and father who will make their child suffer. It's easy to spot it in the parents' eyes, and there are plenty of those types of parents around.

That's how I choose Sally — from seeing the intolerance in her parents' eyes.

But it was a terrible misjudgement. I slipped inside her heart easy enough, but I'm as weak as I ever get in those early stages of a baby's life. So once I realised the mistake I'd made, it was too late to get out — I had to wait until she reached the right age.

That came on her seventh birthday. As did the realisation I'd made another colossal misjudgement.

Sally was too strong for me. I couldn't control her, and she wouldn't let me go. Her harsh upbringing had given her the strength to deny me. No matter how many times I whispered in her mind, it was of no use.

She'd trapped me in her heart.

So all I could do was work on him, the husband. But, of course, he was a man after my own heart. Even so, it took me years.

Until he threw me out of that window.

I was confused at first, to be free after so long. But I could sense fresh vessels around me. They were adults, but it didn't matter. It was all about selecting the right one.

But I had little time.

I think I've made the correct choice for now. I can always change into a different one later. Babies are off the list for a while — I need to revel in my freedom and enjoy myself.

Still, there's one thing I have to do before anything else.

It's time to visit Sally's husband and teach him how the other half lives.

Then, after a few days of torture, I'm sure I'll be back to my usual self.

Then I'll go looking for one of you.

Don't You Forget About Me

'Once I'm gone, you'll be alone and soon forgotten.'

His hands were yellow and wrinkled, with skin reminiscent of ancient papyrus. The homemade tattoos were his own hateful hieroglyphics, fading into an underworld he'd never return from. The clinical antiseptic aroma of the hospital couldn't erode the stench of death flowing from him in waves. The only thing more potent than the smell of his failing body was his whirlwind of hatred for me. It was a mutual loathing.

'I don't need you,' I said.

'You'll be nothing without me,' he replied. 'A failure in everything you've ever done' were the last words to creep out of those torturous lungs. His life was on the brink of the precipice, but all he could do was mock me. And he wasn't wrong. His hollow eyes sunk further into his head, brittle fingers grasping at the bedsheet in the hope he could stop his soul from being dragged down to the warmest of welcomes. So I left before the machines ceased beeping, turning away to extinguish forty years of memories once his withered bones were consumed and crushed into unwanted ashes. I took a short walk from the hospital back to the family home. There was no desire to get my new life started. Not because I didn't want to; I didn't know how to. My father was gone, and so was the hate that had defined me.

My stomach rumbled. I walked to the store and spent my last cash on a tired-looking fish and something masquerading as vegetables. The cod peered at me with watery eyes, its flesh as translucent as my ambitions. It reeked of a fresh carcass, so I drenched it in chilli and garlic. In the kitchen, I sliced it apart with relish, my mind believing the body was his, and this was the garnish to all those times I said I'd leave or kill him.

I had no family, friends, neighbours, or job. Even animals disliked me. Every pet I'd owned had died not long after I'd acquired it or run away the first chance they got. I'd tried being friendly, charming, being generous, but nothing worked.

'You're too much like me,' the old man would say, the only time he acknowledged what he was. Sitting in my room with the isolation threatening to overpower my senses, my fear of being forgotten grew exponentially the more agitated my thoughts became. Religion was alien to me, but I implored for salvation in things I didn't believe in. I scoured the internet for every creed in existence and prayed to multiple gods and goddesses each minute of the day.

Nothing happened, so I switched to the other side of faith, searching through the dark for unnameable creatures and unpronounceable beasts. Nights without sleep transformed the paleness of my skin into a yellow sheen as the whites of my eyes turned red. My nails grew longer as personal hygiene disappeared. My savings shrank at the same rate as my belly, with only the occasional late visit to the store providing me with infrequent nourishment. He'd paid for the house and left me enough money to exist on, but I'd lost the will to live deprived of his vile presence. I would have found it ironic if I'd had the strength to laugh.

Then, one night, it appeared.

'My name is Athaza,' it whispered from the dark corner of my room, eyes shimmering bright red, arcane symbols covering its putrid flesh. 'And I can make sure you're never forgotten.'

It didn't need to coax or deceive me into submission; no contracts were signed or blood spilt. I agreed to its demands without hesitation, embracing its withered hand and knowing my life was transforming. Darkness shifted into illumination in an instant.

People spoke about me in their thousands, my name heard worldwide, and the fear was stripped from my heart. Athaza disappeared, and so had my room. My eyes adjusted to the gloom and saw the endless corpses surrounding me. Death at my feet and all by my bloodied hands. I was the destroyer in human form as they slapped the manacles on my wrists.

'You'll rot in prison,' the officer said to me.

And I grinned.

Happy in the knowledge, I'd never be forgotten.

Not like him.

The one I could never forget.

Thank You!

Thank you, dear reader for purchasing this book.

Many thanks to my wonderful wife for all her support and patience.

Extra special thanks to Karina Gallagher for being a dedicated reader of my work.

Cover design by James, GoOnWrite.com

Mailing List & Free Books!

If you would like to join my mailing list and receive a free eBook then contact me at mail@andrewsfrench.com

About the Author

Andrew French lives amongst faded seaside glamour on the North East coast of England. He likes gin and cats but not together, new music and old movies, curry and ice cream. Slow bike rides and long walks to the pub are his usual exercise, as well as flicking through the pages of good books and the memoirs of bad people.

Find out more at www.andrewsfrench.com

Facebook:

https://www.facebook.com/A-S-French-Author-150145625006018

Twitter:

www.twitter.com/andrewfrench100

Instagram:

www.instagram.com/andrewfrench100

And replies to all his email at mail@andrewsfrench.com

If you have the time, please leave a review at Amazon or Goodreads

Thank you!